Lost in the Woods

LOST
in the
WOODS

& Other Fairy Tales

by

Mark Eddy Smith

themottledspeck.com
TAMWORTH, NH

First Edition

©2018 by Mark Eddy Smith

Cover image: Adobe Stock
Back cover image: iStock

www.themottledspeck.com

ISBN: 978-1-939636-10-2

Table of Contents

Lost in the Woods

(2002)—BASED ON A TRUE STORY FROM 1783

S arah Witcher pouted and tried to force tears, but it was too late: her parents were already walking into the woods. She looked back at the log house, the one where her sister was sitting in front of the fire doing nothing exciting at all, and suddenly she was walking after her parents, toward Uncle Jacob's log house, where Uncle Jacob was sitting in front of the fire waiting to tell her a ghost story.

It was a fine Sunday morning, full of sunlight and butterflies, and surely there were fairies in the forest, just out of sight, waiting to play hide-and-go-seek. She ignored them as long as she could, but it was a long way to Uncle Jacob's, and at some point she stepped off the trail without really noticing. When she did notice, she paid no mind, because it was good to be all by herself in the green and brown and yellow where the fairies lived. When she could no longer pretend she hadn't noticed, she ran back toward the trail.

But the trail wasn't there, and she wasn't sure if it was just to the right or just to the left. She didn't want to cry for help, because she wasn't sure she was lost, and also her parents would be angry. So she sat down quietly under a friendly-looking tree and pretended she was neither lost nor frightened. She crossed her legs, put her hands in her lap and sighed as if to say, "Well, here I am, right where I'm supposed to be. Pretty day, don't you think?"

When she finished weeping, she tried to think what to do. Papa always said that if she ever got lost, she should stay put and he would be along shortly. It was very important that she not move at all, or else he might never catch up with her. She was sure there was something else, something she was forgetting, but though she furrowed her brow until her forehead ached, her memory had nothing further to offer.

She looked around, to keep her mind occupied, taking note of the moss that covered the ground like a green springy quilt, and a lot of little fir trees, and bigger trees behind them, whose names she didn't know. The air smelled fresh and vibrant, heavy with the smell of things waking up from their long winter nap. She breathed in the smells hard through her nose, again and again, until her head felt light. She leaned against the tree and looked up at the lacey branches crisscrossing the blue sky. Without really noticing, she fell asleep.

When she woke up, the tree beneath which Sarah sat was waving its branches furiously, trying to get the black clouds to go away and leave the little girl alone. But black clouds never listen to anybody, and soon their rain was streaming through her hair and behind her ears and alongside her nose. She curled herself into a ball as tight as she could, but the rain was like rivers on her head. Big rivers, like when snow melts in the spring.

She smiled a little, thinking of rivers in her hair, and she thought of how Mama always said she laughed else she'd cry, and she tried to think more queer thoughts about the rain. She thought, maybe there's fish in the rivers in my hair. Papa said that sometimes salmons swam upstream to lay their eggs and when they were finished they were so darn tired they just about died.

Suddenly the thought wasn't so amusing; she didn't want dead fish in her hair. So she shook her head, like a dog will when it wades out from the pond, but then forced herself to stop. If they were dead, they already must have laid their eggs, and she didn't want to shake out the eggs. When they hatched, maybe they'd want to be her friends. If there were a lot of them she'd give them names out of the Bible, like Jacob and Rachel and Abraham and Joseph and Deborah and Isaac and Samson and Noah. Except that Noah made her think of floods, and her smile faded. Except that it also gave her the idea that they could put on Bible plays, her baby salmon friends and her, and they could all play their own people.

She hoped they liked to be rocked, because she was shivering, and she couldn't stop.

Then in the darkness she spied a darker shape, and her heart leapt with hope. "Papa!" she screamed, and would have gotten up, but her legs were asleep. The shape stopped moving, and she put out her arms for a big Papa hug. But when the shape got closer, she saw that it was just a big old dog, all wet and sniffling at her feet. She hugged it anyway, but it wasn't the same as hugging Papa. It was warm, though, and when it curled up around her, she found herself growing so comfortable that she fell asleep once more.

John Witcher smoked his pipe and stared into the fire. Sarah had been missing for two days, and he was remembering how she used to love to play peek-a-boo. She had seemed actually to believe that when her hands were over her eyes she could not be seen. He knew this because when Millie's eyes were covered, Sarah's eyes would grow wide with panic until the hands were swept aside, and the panic turned to rapturous relief. He was thinking, *She might be sitting at the kitchen table right now, giggling under her breath, the game perfected, just waiting for the right moment to yell, 'Peek-a-boo!' and uncover her eyes.* He was thinking, *She'll get a spanking she won't soon forget if I find out she's doing anything of the sort.*

He looked at Millie, her eyes swollen from continuous crying, and reached over to pat her knee. It was hard on a woman, losing a child. It wouldn't do to tell her there'd be more, or that they still had Rebeccah. Best just to let her grieve; she'd get over it in time.

There were 18 families in Warren, New Hampshire, and every one of them had joined in the search or helped out in any way they were able. Even old Joe Patch, who was the first to pioneer the place. Old Joe was afraid Sarah's spirit would haunt the woods if they didn't do their best to find her. Now folks were coming in from the surrounding towns, even from across the Connecticut River. Two days they'd been searching, and although by now it was hopeless, for Millie's sake they intended to continue the search tomorrow. It humbled a man to think that complete strangers would lay off spring planting to help a neighbor find their child.

He listened to the rain on the roof and shuddered, picturing it falling on her unprotected face. Suddenly he was standing, and Millie was looking up at him, expectantly. He turned quickly to the hearth and tapped his pipe against the stones, knocking the plug of tobacco into the ashes. Trying to keep his voice light and steady, he said, "Well, there's some corncobs that need greasing. I'll be back as soon as I'm able."

Millie murmured in response to John's familiar joke. She hadn't slept the past two days, and she hardly felt real anymore. Over and over she was reliving the moment she had asked Rebeccah, their eldest, where Sarah had taken herself off to. She had isolated every emotion that had flashed across Rebeccah's face like lightning across the side of the mountain: surprise, confusion, the glint of humor at the suspicion her parents were having fun at her expense, concern, more confusion, mounting horror and panic at the realization that Sarah had been unaccounted for for hours. All this before Millie had the chance to move from mild curiosity to confusion. Always the scene ended with Rebeccah's quavering voice: "I thought she was with you."

She had always imagined (pridefully, she saw now) that they were blessed. Other folks lost children, some to ill fortune, some to ill health, some to evil spirits, but she had always believed the Witchers immune. She had held on to that belief for two days, and at last she understood it wasn't true. They were cursed, like everyone else in this god-forsaken land, and all their lives would end in grief without solace. It was God's judgment, maybe, though what their sins had been, she couldn't say.

She sat stiff in her rocker, clutching some rag, some plaything of Sarah's, some futile talisman, while her husband wept in the outhouse, great whooping howls. Rebeccah, all but forgotten, hunched by the fire, looked up with alarm. Millie ignored her. It was past time she learned that even a man could be undone by grief.

No doubt he blamed himself for Sarah's wandering off, blamed himself for not teaching her better, for passing on his wanderlust to his child the same way he had passed on his jutting ears. He would pretend it didn't affect him, just like he pretended a stillborn calf was no worse than a lost button, though he wept at night, his back to her, assuming her asleep, and staining his pillow with salt-rimmed tears. Or else he'd excuse himself to the outhouse with a joke.

Wasn't it strange that she could think of no children in all the Bible who died but God sent some prophet, or even His only Son, to raise them from the dead? Nowadays children died on the right and to the left, and where were the prophets with the power to raise them? With weird clarity, as though she were actually hearing the words, she remembered what Jesus had said to Jairus: "It is because of your great faith that I have done this." Was lack of faith the sin for which they were being judged?

She pondered the thought, turning it over like a yard of possibly worth-less cloth, until suddenly she was arrested by a new idea. Could it be that it was not yet too late? A wild hope bloomed awkwardly in her heart as if out of some dun-colored wort that no one would guess might be beautiful. Batting away the fear that this hope, too, might disappoint, she rose and went to the bed, and knelt down to pray. Rebeccah joined her, and Millie imagined their prayers being hastened to heaven on John's rising wails.

From her perch atop the cabin, Rebeccah watched Mr. Heath arrive precisely at noon the following day. She knew it was noon precisely because the sun was shining straight down the chimney she was leaning against and into the cauldron on the fire. The fact that she had never seen him before did not strike her as odd: strangers were coming from all quarters to help search for Sarah. What struck her was that he looked like a madman. He wore his hair loose and it was curly enough to be wild. His clothes seemed to be of uncured leather, and to have been sewn together by a drunk man in the dark. She had seen Indians more fashionably dressed. But he didn't walk like a madman. Despite the shoddiness of his attire, his gait was strong and purposeful, as if his approach were the harbinger of God's wrath. Even from the distance of several rods, his eyes seemed to burn like living coals. She became sure, as he neared, that his gaze would consume her, revealing to all that she was to blame for Sarah's death.

She had been making excuses for herself, but it was true—she had known from the beginning that her parents would never allow little Sarah to accompany them on a Sunday sojourn. It was her own selfish desire for a few hours' solitude that had convinced her otherwise. Her own laziness had kept her from stepping out of doors to make certain all was well. This morning she had awakened on the floor beside her mother, who, though exhausted, was still on her knees, praying hopelessly.

As the man she would later learn was named Mr. Heath stepped up to the door, never spying her on the roof above him, she felt caught between the desire to run away, nevermore to be seen, and to drop a rock from the chimney on his head.

Such was her state of mind when she heard Mr. Heath's first words when her mother answered the door: "Give me some dinner, and I will find your daughter."

Joseph Patch sat with the crowd gathered at the Witcher's kitchen table and studied the stranger, only half-listening to his words. The man had walked from Plymouth, some twenty miles to the south, and the gist of his story was that he had dreamed three times in the night that he had seen the girl under a tree, alive and awake, but Joseph was interested more in Mr. Heath's manner than in his story. He was the kind of man, maybe, for whom one could buy a drink at a tavern, and he'd tell one's fortune. A man like that was looking for another treat. He would have nothing but good to say about the future of anyone buying his drink. Men like that were common enough. On the other hand, there were some who heard God's voice and spoke it true, without regard for how people would take it. These were rare, but it was wise to listen when they crossed one's path, let alone when they had walked a fair distance to deliver their message.

Joseph's dilemma was this: if Mr. Heath was of the former, he should be run out of town, maybe tarred and feathered for trying to bilk a grieving family. But if the latter, it was imperative that someone believe him and act on his words. So he studied him with all the concentration with which he had studied out this land before he pioneered it. The man's getup and wild hair were to be ignored. The volume of his voice, likewise, was of little help. It was a man's eyes that gave him away, darting to the jug, or licking his lips. The good ones would take a push to betray themselves like that, and Joseph Patch figured the time had come for a push. Still, he knew he'd best be careful. If the man was the genuine article, he might be offended, and call down God's curse upon the town for its unbelief. He cleared his throat.

"Would you care for a swallow, Mr. . . . Heath was it?"

The silence was sudden, and the man's eyes turned toward him slowly. They were ominous eyes, but Joseph Patch had faced down a painter once, a cat almost as big as himself, and that at night, and both of them caught unawares. For most of a minute no one cleared their throat or shuffled their feet.

At last, with an effort, Joseph spoke again. "I reckon you could use some company—someone who knows the woods." His words sounded thick, as though he himself had been drinking, but the man's glowering eyes softened, and he felt a great weight lift, though he hadn't marked the heaviness before. Mr. Heath smiled, like sunrise on a mountain, and everyone laughed, though doubtless they knew no reason for it. "I'd be glad of your company, sir," said Mr. Heath, just as handsome as you please. For Joseph Patch, soon to be sixty-seven years old, it was as though he was a child again, and his father asking him on his first hunting trip, and he, too, found himself laughing.

Later in her life, Sarah would be called upon often to tell of her adventure. She enjoyed the tale, but in truth, she remembered little of it. She had spent three nights under a tree in the later part of spring, and but for the kindness of a passing dog, she surely would have died. Every night it had returned to her, curled up around her, and kept her warm and protected. Although this had not seemed strange at the time, she was often surprised, looking back, at how trusting she had been. She had never been afraid of it, nor had she ever doubted that it would return the following night. She had never thought to wonder whose dog it was—as far as she was concerned, it had been hers. Of the days she had spent keeping close to the tree, amusing herself with daydreams, she remembered only that she had been hungry and, after the puddles from the first night's rain dried up, thirsty as well. The only other memory she had was of her parents, upon her return in the arms of Joseph Patch.

Her mother, upon seeing her, had simply fainted. Her father had remained standing, fuming silently, and that had disturbed her, but the townsfolk, who loved this part of the tale better than any other, noticed something Sarah likely never would have. They were fond of teasing her father for it: He was smoking so furiously that the bowl of his pipe had burst into flame.

Sometimes, even when she was old and had grandchildren to dote upon, she would find herself lying in bed after a difficult day, and the smell and the warmth of the dog that had saved her life would surround her, and sorrow would well in her breast, for not even her husband had ever made her feel so loved.

Joseph Patch told a different story, though never in Sarah's presence: "T'wa'nt no *dog* tracks, I can tell you that much. . . ."

Near dusk, the evening after Sarah's rescue by Mr. Heath and Joseph Patch, a black bear loped toward a tree. When he found the spot empty, he stopped abruptly, sending ripples coursing through his pelt. Motionless for several minutes, he then rose to his hind legs and sniffed the wind, peering about with nearsighted eyes. He could smell the two men who had come for the girl cub, and his nose wrinkled with disgust. He dropped to all fours and for several more minutes simply stared at the ground. At last he lumbered to the tree, curled up at the roots where Sarah Witcher had sat, and tried, unsuccessfully, to sleep.

Bears All

(1994)

Edward C. Passover had turned off the trail to find some blackberries when God turned him into a bear. He wasn't sure exactly when it had happened. One moment he'd been picking berries one by one and popping them into his mouth, the next he'd been drawing clusters of berries to his snout and munching off most of the leaves. Not until he trundled back to the path did he realize he was no longer human. Immediately he was filled with a deep sorrow, for all of his dreams were now lost. Peering around nearsightedly, he snuffled the strange new smells, until at last, resigned, he wandered away from the path to find more berries.

Years later, in the latter part of Autumn, when the rains were not unbearably cold, Edward came upon a little girl, sitting with her back against a tree. When she saw him she smiled, and held out her arms. He came nearer and snuffled her face. She put her arms around his neck and squeezed very tightly. He lay down on his side and offered his warm dry chest to her. She snuggled in and promptly fell asleep. All night he held his arm out over her, keeping her dry. In the morning the rain stopped, and Edward got up and left. He returned in the evening to find her still sitting under the tree. "Nice doggy," she said, as she hugged him and petted his nose. Again he spent the night, and the next night, and the night after, keeping her warm and dry. On the fifth night, the place where she had been smelled powerfully of two men. He never saw the little girl again, though he thought of her often and missed her terribly.

In the spring of his seventh year as a bear, Edward saw a she-bear rubbing against a tree. His heart rose within him, for she was very beautiful. In time they mated, and she bore four cubs. For a time, Edward was content. With winter, however, came a strange restlessness. He woke often in his den, and, though it was bitter cold, he wandered far and wide, scratching trees and dirtying snow. Often, in the evenings, he would find himself on a mountainside, looking down over some village or town. As the lights came on, their glow would fill him with longing.

At last, spring returned, and his wife began to nuzzle him affectionately. He found, however, that he was now repulsed by her ursine bulk, and the thought of mating filled him with loathing. Still, he could not bear to hurt her, so he nuzzled her back, and hugged her, and tried to be kind. When at last he could stand it no longer, he cried out, in agony of soul. Immediately stepped a man from behind a tree. His wife fell on her face before him, and Edward himself bowed his head in shame. Jesus stepped closer and scratched him behind the ear.

"Edward," he said, and Edward was human again.

Jesus then went to his wife, and lay down beside her. In a moment, Edward saw that he was weeping, and that the great bear that had been his wife wept also. The weeping continued for a long time before Jesus rose to his knees and gently put his hand upon her head. "Brunhilde," he said, and she was a lovely buxom woman with wild blonde hair. Jesus touched her lips and breathed on her, and in this way gave her speech. He took her hand and reached out, took Edward's hand, and drew their hands together. He told them to go into the village, where a kindly widow would give them clothes and a place to stay. Then he disappeared into the forest. The couple walked into the village and found everything just as Jesus had said.

Over dinner the wise old widow told them of the dream she had had concerning their arrival. In the dream, Jesus had shown her Brunhilde's grandmother, who was born in Sweden, and was turned into a bear by a wicked magician for spurning his affections. The magician had sold her to the ringmaster of a circus, who had put her on a ship to America. The ship was wrecked some fifteen miles off the coast of Maine. She had barely survived the swim, and once ashore, had been unable to escape the affections of the native bears. She had given birth to Brunhilde's mother, who in turn had given birth to Brunhilde. "And what of *my* children?" cried Brunhilde, greatly distressed. At that moment, a knocking was heard at the door. When they opened it, they found four children, less than a year old, wrapped in linen cloths, sleeping peacefully on the doorstep.

The Mouse & the Dragon

(1988)

Once upon a time, something happened.

I was sitting outside my mouse hole, gnawing on a kernel of corn, watching a dragon circle high above, glinting in the late August sun. I was thinking how beautiful the dragon was, and how scared I was lest it should see me and be upon me before I could leap backward into my hole. I wished that I were as beautiful, and could fly.

Then the dragon stopped circling and stretched its neck out full. I cowered further into the entrance of my hole, but the dragon plummeted to a different corner of the field. I watched, mesmerized, as it dove straight down, head first, and at the last moment, faster than my eyes could register, pulled up, flicked its talons, and rose again, a small grey mouse added to the five it had already caught on the ends of its talons.

I couldn't help noticing how graceful the red and gold creature looked as it soared upward, wings outstretched, exulting in the joy of flight. As it floated away, towards the mountain rising above the forest, I tried to mourn the loss of six more of my neighbors, but found instead that I was trying to imagine how the earth must look from such an altitude.

That night I dreamed I flew toward the mountain, pursuing the killer dragon. I would avenge my fallen brothers. I felt exhilarated by the cold air streaming past my face. Adrenaline surged through my body as I topped the mountain's peak and beheld a multitude of dragons dancing through the air.

Fear thrilled me, and I paused, prepared to flee, but then the dragons looked at me, all of them at once, and cheered. For a moment, I hovered, confused. Than I looked at my feet and found that there were eleven mice squirming on the ends of my enormous talons.

When I awoke the next morning, the thrill of flight was still with me, but I had to spend a long time reconstructing my dream before I could remember the final scene. My shame could not overshout my desire for the dream to come true.

As winter approached, thoughts of dragons faded, and I turned my mind toward stocking my larder. I spent the winter sleeping and eating, and generally doing nothing at all. My mind was too lethargic to wander very far. Nevertheless, I would often wake up, late at night, despising the slight weight that held me underground, and trying in vain to remember how my dream of flight had felt. I yearned for spring and the lightening of my mood, if not my body. It was long in coming.

When at last the snows did melt from over my hole, and water trickled steadily into the recess I had dug for it, I ventured out and stuck my head into the freshening breeze. The sky seemed to beg me to leap up and keep it company, but my body held me fast.

As spring ripened, the younger mice started venturing into the woods, trying vainly to satisfy a desire to see the world. I, who once thought myself too old for such wanderlust, found myself venturing more deeply into the forest than any of them. I once walked all the way to the foot of the mountain which separated me from my dragons. I yearned to attempt the climb, but, fearing that I might get lost, I reluctantly returned to the field.

On the first day of summer, I woke up around midnight and felt that I could wait no longer. My sirenic dream was calling.

I crawled out of the leaf pile that I used as a summer bed, trying to clear the pond scum from my mind, and walked into the night.

The moon was three-quarters full, and traced every blade of grass and every grain of dirt separately and distinctly. I didn't like the night, as a rule, but it was beautiful just the same.

A tree frog peeped shrilly, followed by another, and another, until an entire chorus burst into song. I took comfort in their presence, feeling that if any danger approached, the frogs would immediately cease. I took a few breaths of the warm night air to relax myself, then set off in the direction of the woods.

I reached the edge of the field in a few minutes. It was darker than I had expected. The trees looked taller and more imposing, and what little moonlight filtered in caused the forest to look more eerie. For a moment, I didn't think I would be able to walk in.

But I couldn't turn back. My only desire was to watch the dragons as I had in my dream, and in order to do that, I had to walk into the woods. I took another deep breath, held it, and strode into the trees.

Almost immediately, I stopped striding, and settled for creeping. I didn't like the way the leaves and pine needles felt under my paws. They were damp, and they rustled, and I kept imagining that they were lying on top of slugs and centipedes and spiders.

The distant hoot of an owl reminded me of a much more real and frightening danger, which I had almost forgotten.

I was suddenly terrified. There was no place to hide, no place to run, and at any moment, the silent talons of an owl might grab me and wing me to their nest. My urge to fly was not so desperate.

From then on, I kept very close to the bases of trees. As I walked, however, being as wary as possible, through the endless woods, I began to tire. Sleep and waking played tug-of-war with my eyelids, and occasionally my mind would skip over a few moments, so that time seemed suddenly to leap forward without me. Soon, I had forgotten to be scared of owls, and was walking in a straight line, in what I hoped was the right direction.

When the sun rose, I found that I was walking uphill. I was ascending the mountain.

I slept under a rock for most of the day, continuing my journey only after the sun had passed over the mountain. I wasn't sure why I chose the night to do my hiking, except that that was when my desire to see dragons was strongest. Besides, I hoped to reach the top of the mountain by dawn, so that the sun would be at my back as I looked over.

It was harder going that night. The ground was rocky and the uphill grade eventually began to cause a steady burning in my legs. The night was chilly, and the air rasped in my lungs. I kept myself going solely on the belief that the peak would bring the end of my quest, and I could rest there as long as I wanted. I tried to hold the vision from my dream before me as I climbed.

The sun was high above me when I reached a disappointing pinnacle. The mountain never broke out of the trees, and I could see nothing more than thirty feet away save sky.

I found another rock, this one with a fair-sized crack in it, and spent the day there, sleeping a deep and exhausted sleep.

When I woke, dawn was once more near. I decided that the mountain could redeem itself if I could find a ledge or huge boulder from which I could overlook the trees. I stretched my aching body, and began the descent towards the other side of the mountain.

After an hour or two of searching, I emerged from the trees, and was greeted by a spectacular, but also disappointing view.

The valley stretched for miles, dotted here and there with fields, and ending with the most spectacular range of mountains I had ever dreamed of seeing.

The nearer mountains were a deep green, fading to blue and white and purple in the barely discernible distance. Sunlight glanced off distant snows, brilliant in the faint light of the mountain's shadow. I was awed by the existence of such a majestic view so close to my little field, and I marveled at the tiny scope of my life.

Suddenly, I noticed a large dot in the sky, getting steadily larger. Something was flying straight at me, and in a moment, I realized it was a dragon. I scampered back into the trees and cowered behind a large pine, but the dragon continued towards me. I glanced up at the tree, wondering if it would be able to shield me, then glanced at the dragon again. To my relief, I noticed that it was not flying at me at all, but to a spot further down the mountain.

When it disappeared, I padded back to the ledge and looked over. I could make out nothing discernible, and suddenly, I was looking for a way around the ledge, and further down the mountain.

Some time later, I was wandering around near the base of the mountain, having found not the least trace of the dragon. By now, I wasn't even sure why I was looking. I didn't really want to see a dragon this close up.

A sudden drop of water hit me in the nape of the neck and immediately seeped into my coat. I scrinched my neck to the sudden cold and, looking up, noticed that the sky had grown dark with clouds.

The droplets quickly grew in intensity until my fur was matted and my whiskers were continually tickled by the rain. After a while, they began to feel slightly numb, and in the near darkness of the storm, I bumped into many a rock and branch that I should have known were there. The tickling sensation spread to my nose, and I felt constantly on the verge of a sneeze. I decided it was time to find shelter.

The cave that suddenly loomed on the side of the mountain was much too large. It was about the right size for the dragon I had been following. Nevertheless, I was too thoroughly miserable to do anything but sneak a little way in and pray that the dragon wouldn't notice.

To my surprise, the cave was not only dry, but warm. As I huddled against the wall, about three feet in, I could feel the moisture being drawn from my skin. The cave was too dark, however, to see very far inside.

Within five minutes, I was fast asleep.

I was lying on a pile of leaves when I woke, and I wondered how I had gotten home. I wondered if I had dreamed my entire adventure.

Then I heard a voice that assured me that I could not be in my hole, since the voice itself was easily the size of a mountain.

Its depth and timbre reminded me of distant thunder. It said, simply, "Good morning. My name is Sue." With a soft 'flump', like the sound of a rock landing in a pile of loose sand, a tiny flame appeared, revealing the nature of the creature that addressed me.

In the flickering shadows cast by the flame, a large, red and gold dragon was grinning broadly.

I fainted.

When I came to, the cave was brilliantly lit with flaming branches ranged along the wall. The dragon was curled up in the middle of the floor and was peering at me through half-lidded eyes. "Again I say, 'good morning.' As long as your heart holds out, you are in no danger. You are welcome to stay, if you wish, or leave, if you prefer, but I would be pleased if you would remain long enough to entertain me with the story of your travels."

The red along her back was the color of the sun, as it sinks over the horizon after a humid day. The yellow along her belly was the color of the sun, as it rises, spreading warmth over a late summer dawn. Her eyes were the color of the sun in the glory of noontime, and I could barely stand to look at them.

Her tail was longer and narrower than her neck, and ended in a broad, leaf-shaped spike. Her skin looked tough but pliant, with a texture like a turtle's shell. Her wings, though folded, looked powerful and iridescent.

Her legs were beneath her, and that was just as well, as I didn't want to be reminded of her talons. A snake's tongue slipped through her sharp, grinning teeth.

I was enthralled.

"You *can* talk, can't you?"

"What's the most mice you ever caught at one time?" I asked, much to my own surprise.

Sue's laugh was rich and booming, like thunder that's directly overhead. "I've never played Mausjammer, my friend. Besides, there isn't enough room for me to get the proper altitude to puncture you."

It took a moment to figure out why I was confused, but after a pause, I said, "What's 'Mausjammer'?"

Sue's eyes narrowed. "What do you mean, 'What's—'? Surely you—
Why, the puck might just as well ask, 'What's hockey?' or the bull's-eye,
'What's archery?' Mausjammer is the dragons' national pastime. Mausjammer is a game, in which one attempts to 'puncture' as many mice as possible
in the shortest amount of time. If I've correctly deduced where you come
from, then yours is one of the practice fields. You are one of the pieces in
the game. Surely you knew this?"

"A game? " I asked, dreamily. "What's the record?"

"I believe it's ten," said Sue.

"Then I broke the record," I said, in a tiny whisper. I walked away and
tried not to think.

Before long, I found myself wandering through a tunnel, I took the
various twists and turns at random, feeling too lost mentally to worry
about becoming so physically.

I wandered for half an hour or so, breathing the cold, wet air, wondering,
despite my best efforts not to, what my dream had meant. At last, upon
turning one final corner, I was confronted with Sue. I'm not sure how she
got in front of me, but she didn't give me time to ask.

"You need to go flying," she said. Then she winked at me and nodded
her head, and I found myself lifted off the floor by invisible means. I floated
over her head and alit between her shoulders. She began to unfold her
wings, though there clearly wasn't enough room, and suddenly there was
plenty of room and we were outside in the sunshine about a mile in the air
and my heart was pounding furiously.

"Magic can be a wonderful thing," said Sue, looking over her shoulder
and grinning. "So long as you use it wisely."

Then she began to fly.

Down she plummeted, her wings held close. Up she soared, wings
outstretched, her body curved backwards. She glided, she banked, she
swooped, while I clung between her shoulder blades, giddy and slightly
nauseous, wishing it would stop, and praying it would never end.

It went on for another ten minutes, and then she folded her wings, and we were back in the cave, and I was lifted off her shoulders and back onto the ground.

"Supper's ready, if you want it," said Sue, as she turned and walked away.

Dazed and slightly dizzy, I weaved after her, to the central chamber.

In the middle of the chamber, the carcass of a gigantic, yellow and black striped cat festered, with its rib cage opened up and smelling. I nearly passed out until I noticed the kernels of corn that were piled up about six feet away. These looked so succulent and yellow that I nearly passed out again as my forgotten hunger suddenly leapt up and started drooling.

"Good corn, good meat; good God, let's eat!" said Sue, and I stumble-sprinted to the pile and began to devour it.

When I finished, having eaten six kernels, I looked up at Sue, who laughed.

"You need a mirror," she said. "Mirror!"

And suddenly I was standing in front of myself, bits of corn hanging from my slavering jaw. I yelped and threw myself backwards.

"Dismissed," laughed Sue, and the apparition faded. "I'm afraid you're going to be doing rather a lot of that in the days to come," said Sue. "Yelping and throwing yourself backwards, that is. Magic and technology are somewhat startling entities."

I had almost recovered myself, though I was still trembling, when Sue said, "Oh dear, you seem to have lost control of some of your more basic muscle control in your fright. But not to worry, it won't take but a moment to clean."

I looked behind me and was ashamed to see a long black turd lying innocently on the floor. My face got very hot, and I started to mumble something, but Sue said, "Shit!" in a loud and commanding voice, and the turd got up and marched outside. I stared at it with an odd fascination, then started to laugh.

The laugh began with brief exhalations through my nose and what felt like a sad/comic expression on my face, then my mouth opened, and the laugh found a voice, and then I was rolling on my back, with tears streaming through my fur, screaming with laughter. I was laughing, not only at the marching turd, but at everything that had happened in the last three days. All the effort of climbing the mountain, Sue's voice in the darkness when I had thought the mountain was talking to me, even, or perhaps especially, the mirror trick and my shame.

When the laughter left me, reluctantly, and I was only giggling softly, I suddenly realized that I felt good. Good in a way that I hadn't felt since I was a child. I felt clean—purified. I wanted to fly again.

"You laugh well," said Sue.

Eventually, I sobered, and Sue repeated her request to hear the tale of my travels.

Starting with my desire to see the dance of the dragons, and ending with falling asleep inside Sue's cave, I obliged her.

"How would you like to take another ride?" asked Sue, when I finished.

I said that I would like it very much.

The city I had seen in my dream was on the other side of the mountains I had seen from the ledge. As we flew, Sue explained that Svetlavia was the capitol city of the dragons and was something over seven thousand years old. That's all she had time to say, because we were suddenly flying up and over the mountain, and the sight was fantastic.

We crested the mountain just like I had in my dream, but reality was even more spectacular. Dragons that looked no bigger than sparrows were weaving and twisting their way over and around the city. My dream was fulfilled.

The city itself was like nothing I had ever seen. It was built around a gigantic hole in the ground, into and out of which dragons by the score were flying like bees. Great colorful mounds of earth and stone reared over each other, hosting more dragon traffic. I wanted to see more.

"Let's get closer," I said.

"I can't," said Sue. She spread her wings, and we flew back to her cave.

When we returned, Sue set me down and said, "You know, you have yet to tell me your name."

"It's Mike," I said.

"Good," said Sue, and she spread her wings again and disappeared.

Three days passed before she returned, and during that time, I found plenty of things to worry about. I worried that there was some reason for her inability to enter the city that went beyond the fact that she was carrying a mouse. I worried that that reason had something to do with her continued absence. I worried that she wouldn't come back.

The afternoon of the third day, I ate the last of the corn that Sue had provided, and began to worry where my next meal would come from, but finally, she reappeared.

She looked tired, but happy.

"Still here, eh? I thought you might run out on me while I was away, but I'm glad you didn't. I brought you a few more kernels of corn."

She didn't mention her disappearance until after supper. I had one of the kernels, and she ate another large cat, though this one was tawny, and had lots of hair on its head. When she had been eating the orange, striped one, I had been too busy devouring my own food to watch her, but this time, though I tried to find something else to look at, my gaze was constantly drawn to her meal.

I was surprised to find that she ate very quietly and neatly, with a minimum of rending flesh. Her teeth were so sharp that she had an easier time eating the cat than I had eating corn. She was almost dainty. It was an unnerving sight just the same.

When she finished, she looked up at me and smiled. "A little tough, but I always get a kick out of eating lions. They come from Africa, mostly. Beautiful place." She paused, and stared, until I felt uncomfortable, then said, "I'm sorry I couldn't take you into the city. It's a singularly wonderful place . . .

"I'm afraid I'm not well liked there. Nobody likes a doomsayer. Some people hate them. At the moment, its none of your concern, but the longer you stay here, the greater the risk that it will become yours.

"I'm not asking you to leave, of course. On the contrary, I would love to have you stay; you're the first friend I've had in a long, long time. I just wanted you to know that things could get a little . . . hectic in the days to come, that's all. Anyway, it's been a long three days, and I simply must get to bed. Goodnight."

"Goodnight," I said, puzzled as usual, and went to sleep myself.

The next morning, I was jolted from sleep by a booming roll of thunder that seemed to be erupting from within my own head. When I realized the thunder was talking, I hurried out of bed and crept cautiously to the mouth of the cave.

Sue was already there, looking up into the sky and fuming. Following her gaze, I saw nine dragons hovering in Canada goose formation. The dragon at the apex was the largest, and was producing the thunderous voice. Even when my ears adjusted to the volume, though, I could only catch portions of what the thunderer was saying.

Two of the words I did catch were "traitor," and "death." I think they were repeated several times. The dragon also seemed to want Sue to come with it.

When the speech was over, and the echoes had reverberated away, Sue quietly and distinctly said, "Fuck you," and marched into the cave.

"I wouldn't stand too close to the door," she said, and lifted me in front of her. A moment later, the thunder was replaced by lightening and the area in front of the cave burst into flame. Although Sue took the brunt of the hot air that suddenly battered its way in, I felt as though I were being roasted by the heat. "It looks like trouble got here faster than I expected," she said.

When the flames died away, after an hour or so, the dragons were gone. Two of the pine trees closest to the cave were still on fire, but the flames weren't spreading beyond them.

"That was the Tribunal," said Sue. "Once a proud and compassionate institution, now a group of aged headhunters, always on the lookout for more heads. The end of our millennium is very near."

The explanation meant nothing to me, but I got the idea that the situation was dire.

That night, Sue and I slept in one of the innermost chambers. The next morning, explosions ripped the air, and Thunder had a few more words to say. When the Tribunal left, we investigated the damage and found that most of the cave had been turned into a crater.

"Just what is it they want from you?" I asked.

"My life," said Sue. "And I believe the time has come for me to do something about it. Would you like to witness an insurrection?"

"What's a—," I asked.

"Come on; I'll show you," she replied.

She lifted me onto her back and we flew once more to Svetlavia.

The city looked exactly the same, but this time Sue did not stop at the top of the mountain. She was flying so fast that I could make out no new details as we closed in, and Sue only went faster as we approached.

By the time we reached the city's edge, the landscape was a blur. How she managed to avoid hitting one of the thousands of dragons that were flying around is beyond me, but when we were directly above the hole, among the thickest traffic, she made a ninety-degree turn and plunged into the darkness.

For a long time, the only indication I had of movement was the rush of air that streamed past, and the fact that my ears were popping. I tried to reassure myself of Sue's trustworthiness and sanity.

When at last I noticed a pinprick of light in the darkness, it immediately resolved into a massive portal through which we proceeded to hurtle. Only then did Sue begin to slow.

The scene that resolved around us was exactly like a honeycomb. Great, hexagonal cells ranged as far as I could see on either side. There seemed no end to them, either above or ahead. I had no interest in trying to catch a glimpse of the floor. Though most of the cells were plugged, I didn't imagine they were filled with honey.

"This is the prison," said Sue, "and in a moment, you will see the guards."

An ear-piercing shriek filled the air, and in the next moment, we were completely surrounded by a phalanx of dragons wearing scarlet bands around their heads.

Sue hovered in place as the dragons slowly constricted their sphere. Disconcertingly, she started to tremble. Then she started to glow.

"Just a few more moments," whispered Sue.

Dimly, I realized that she wasn't so much trembling as thrumming. Power seemed to be building within her. I was too terrified just then to wonder why I was there.

"Uh-oh," said Sue, and, abruptly, the thrumming stopped, as did the up and down motion of her wings. In the ensuing silence, I forced myself to open my eyes.

Sue was no longer glowing, or moving at all. She just hung suspended, frozen, while the phalanx of guards backed away. Finally, I looked along Sue's neck. A golden bowl was upended on her head.

I wish I could tell you what was running through my mind at that moment, but I was too busy running recklessly alongside the scales of her neck to pay much attention to what I was thinking. I just somehow knew that the bowl had to be dislodged.

It was much too big for me to lift, but I grabbed hold of the rim anyway, and lifted with everything in me. Ordinarily, I wouldn't have stood a chance, but after walking up and down a mountain, my legs had grown abnormally strong. Also, fear, and something hotter within me that may have been rage, lent strength enough to my legs and paws that the bowl moved. It was only high enough to admit a single kernel of corn, but apparently it was enough. Sue shook her head, and the bowl bounced into the air. Unfortunately, so did I.

I fell silently, with nothing below me but darkness. Above me, Sue recommenced to glow, only twice as brightly as before, and the thrumming I had noticed before was in the very air. The guards were in disarray, and the whole tableau was growing smaller by the instant.

That's when Sue exploded. For an instant the honeycomb cells were lit as if by sunlight, but even as the golden walls glinted, they faded away, and as the brightness dimmed, each cell released a dragon, who flew upwards, streaming fire from their jaws, so that I seemed to be falling through a conflagration. The wind from their wings blew me every which way but up. I had time to think that my imminent death was easily worth the unimaginable glory of that sight when Sue suddenly appeared beside me, falling at the same sped, and grinning her toothy grin. "How do you like the joy of flight? she asked.

I opened my mouth and screamed.

Sue casually maneuvered herself underneath me until I was effectively sitting between her shoulders.

She slowed to a stop, then soared upwards. As we rose, I had time to study the spectacle above us. Unfortunately, I have nothing to compare it to. Flames every color of the rainbow were shooting in every direction as the freed prisoners engaged their guards in battle.

Sue began to laugh. "Behold the reaping of the whirlwind," she yelled.

She continued to fly casually towards the exit portal, which was guarded by half a dozen desperate-looking guards. When they saw Sue, they shouted and tried to surround her, but Sue took a deep breath, blew a mighty blast of fire, and sped on through.

When the darkness once more protected us, she picked up speed. I clung to her scales as well as I could, while the wind tried to pull my hair out by its follicles. At long last, we shot through the city's giant hole and high into the air, until the city was too small to distinguish.

"Well, that was more exciting than I had anticipated," said Sue. "It required every ounce of my magic, and finally hung on the strength and courage of a mouse, but we actually pulled it off. The city will either be reborn or destroyed. Either way, it will be a marked improvement.

"I apologize for the mortal peril; I had fully expected to fly in and out without incident. I certainly wasn't anticipating the Helm of Hrim. It's a purely mythic artifact that turns magic in upon itself. I never dreamed it actually existed. If not for your quick thinking and strong limbs, I would simply have imploded, no doubt taking you with me, but otherwise causing no harm. So, thank you."

"Don't mention it," I said, breathlessly.

Later, as we stood in the middle of the crater that had been Sue's home, she said, "This was a good home, I lived here for 863 years. It won't be easy leaving it."

"Where will go?"

"Well, as I think I mentioned, Africa is a beautiful place, with lots of lions and other toothsome feasts. Ample room for a dragon to spread her wings. Would you like to come along?"

I laughed. "I think I've had more than enough excitement to last a poor little field mouse a lifetime." Then I turned serious. "But I'll miss you."

"And I you, my friend."

I watched her for a long time after she had become too small to see.

That was two years ago. Since that time, I have done little save scratch out this story. I eat, I sleep, occasionally, I dream, but nothing ever really happens. Now that my tale is complete, I am faced with spending the rest of my life doing nothing exciting save dream.

I refuse to accept that fate. Tonight is the first night of summer, and the moon is nearly full. I don't know where Africa is, but I know in which direction my dragon flew. I will start from her cave on the other side of the mountain and follow her to Africa. If I die before I reach there, then at least I will have died in action, rather than in my hole. But who knows? Perhaps I will actually find her, and we'll be able to spend the rest of our lives together, having grand adventures.

Once upon a time, I flew. Perhaps, in the magical realm of Africa, I will fly again.

The Beginning . . .

How the Bumblebee Learned to Fly

(1996)—BEFORE SCIENTISTS WORKED OUT BUMBLEBEE AERODYNAMICS

In the latter days of Solomon, when God was wishing the king had asked for monogamy, the *Deus Omnia Rerum* (that is, the God of All Creation), began tinkering with his creatures, both to confound the king's vaunted wisdom and to get his own mind off the number and variety of queens. Among the results of his endeavors were a type of badger that exceedingly stank, a type of cat that, while continuing to hate every creature but itself, yet desired to be a pet, and a type of beaver that was also a duck. But most puzzling of all was a bee who was too big for its wings.

This bee was content to wander the earth, shimmying up flower stems and industriously collecting pollen. It used its wings to cool itself off and, though it admitted that flying must be a wonderful thing, it never complained nor envied other bees in its heart. Occasionally, for the amusement of friends and small children, it would use its wings to lift itself up onto its hind legs and strut around in mock self-importance. But sometimes, if its friends laughed too heartily or for too long, the bee would get a little sad.

One day, a little girl, who hadn't any parents, asked the bee why it didn't fly but only bumbled about on the ground. As the bee had no answer, and Mathilda (for that was the little girl's name) could think of only one person wise enough to answer, she scooped up the bee and immediately skipped to the palace.

"I am the Queen of Sheba," she announced to the guards, her hands clasped grandly in front of her, "and I demand to see the King!" As the guards paid no attention, she marched right past them and into the palace. She encountered the king in an antechamber, lying naked and having his back rubbed. He appeared to be fast asleep.

Drawing a breath and composing her features, Mathilda approached in a stately manner. She put her mouth quite close to the royal ear and shouted, "Your Highness!" then jumped back when the king looked up in alarm.

"What?" he said. "Oh. Hello, there." He smiled, a little bleary-eyed, then frowned when he noticed her hands. *Oh*, he said to his wisdom, *One of them*.

"I suppose," he said, addressing Mathilda, "that you want me to guess what you're holding."

Mathilda screwed up her eyes and shook her head

"You want me to judge which hand should let go of the other?"

Mathilda shook her head more emphatically.

The king frowned. "You want me to order the guards to cut you in half!" Even he had to admit he was getting crotchety in his old age.

Mathilda continued to swing her head from side to side, but it was hard for the king to tell whether she did so now in denial of his guesses or simply to enjoy the swishing of her hair.

"Well, then, what is it?" said the king.

Mathilda stopped swinging her head and bit her bottom lip. She glanced from left to right, then skated her bare feet closer to the king.

"Why would God," she whispered, opening her hands before the king's face, "make a bee that's too bumbledy to fly?"

The king peered at the overlarge insect in the little girl's hands and frowned using only his eyebrows. "Well, it is rather big," he said, "And unshapely. And it's wings are a mite too short, but," and here he looked sharply at Mathilda, "are you quite certain it can't fly at all?"

The bee stepped forward nervously onto Mathilda's finger and tremblingly bowed. With all its might it buzzed, lifting itself slowly onto its sturdy hind legs and then stepped from the finger and plunged straight to the floor.

"Good God!" said the king, sitting up in alarm. (The masseuse was hasty to cover him.) In a trice he was down on his hands and knees and studying the slightly dazed insect. "It really can't fly," mused the king, as he studied the bee up and down. "Why should that be?"

For fifteen minutes and more the king studied, and suddenly he brought his hand down *slap!* onto the floor beside the bee. Though it flinched, it made no move to fly. Fifteen minutes and more and more, and the king, in frustration, blew with all his might, but the bee did no more than roll. He chased it, yelling, and the bee buzzed along, running terrified on its thickly hind legs, but though the king threatened to crush it, it didn't so much as hop. At last the king buried his face in his elbows and thought and thought (and thought and thought). He kicked his feet, he rubbed his face, and, at last, looking up, with tears in his anguished eyes, he strained to remember what was usually said when one couldn't come up with the answer.

Now Mathilda, if you must know the truth, was pleased by the trouble she'd caused. But the bee was a humbler sort, and its heart grew heavy at the king's defeat. *Dear God,* it said in its tiny heart, *I don't care if I never do fly. You gave me wings to cool me down and make me funny for friends. And that's more than any bee has a right to ask for. But this is king Solomon, who for your sake, and for the sake of your people, asked nothing for himself but only wisdom to rule your people well. For his sake, well, couldn't you maybe make me fly, just a little, just this once?*

And the *Deus ex Machina* (that is, the God who Intervenes), though pleased for Mathilda and grieved for the king, was moved most of all by the bee. "Flap your wings, little Bumble," whispered God to its heart, "and while you buzz, I will lift you." So the bee flapped its wings and was lifted, and as its feet left the floor, and it flew up to Mathilda's nose, it praised God, and hummed for joy, because until then it hadn't known what a marvel it is to fly.

"Aha!" said the king, "I was right all along!" and he stood up and grinned through his tears.

"Oh bee! You really can fly," screamed Mathilda, jumping and waving her arms. (She waved them as hard as she could, but God wouldn't lift her up—she got into enough mischief as it was).

And the bee flew loop-de-loops and barrel rolls, and complicated dances through the cool, palace air.

And from that day till this, if a bumblebee wishes to fly, it just buzzes its wings and it prays. And the Lord God Almighty, who made it for sport, gently carries it wherever it wishes.

The Christmas Serpent

I was born on Christmas Eve—I mean the real one.
My mother carved the moment out of stone.
My Little Beast of the Apocalypse, she called me, as if it made her
     proud.
I watched the baby Jesus grow up strong.
I saw his faithful love move more than mountains.
I was there when he met Legion, that band of demons that begged
     mercy.
He cast them into pigs at their request.
I thought, *If he can pity demons, might he even accept . . . me?*

One Friday morn I watched rough hands lay a cross upon his shoulders
And march him towards a place they called the Skull.
I must admit I watched with glee
for heaven's might to blast them.
They nailed him high, the sky grew dark—
I shut my eyes and waited—
But nothing happened.
I searched the sky for angels;
There were none there to be found
until at last I bellowed forth to save him;
only then a flaming sword appeared and held my wrath at bay.
"What are you doing?" I cried. "We can't just let him die!"
The sword began to droop, the face behind it writhed in pain,
Tears welled up in shining eyes that glanced at Christ with yearning,
But the sword remained.
At three o'clock the Lord of heaven died.
Eli! Eli lema sabachthani!

Can you hear it?

I was born on Christmas Eve; I saw the Savior crucified.
I spent that Sabbath grieving at his tomb.
But then, on Sunday morning, that same angel who opposed me
asked if I might like a chance to move a mountain.
In sorrow and confusion I was slow in my reply,
but the angel's glowing face seemed almost giddy.
He pointed to the stone that sealed the grave.
I rolled it back, expecting they would take him up to heaven,
and sad I was to see his body leave.
But lo! While angels all around me fell down crashing to their knees,
The man inside walked forth into the dawn.
He looked a little weary, but he had the strength to smile,
And he threw his arms around my neck and laughed.
That laugh!

I was the first of the born-again dragons.

Thurnglad's Meadbowl

(1994)

Thurnglad brooded often in the mead hall, yearning for war and winter's end. Folks around him strained to be cheerful, singing and boasting as if the world were not dead. They would cease their bellowings and beg him for aid when the wolves descended and prowled the woods. As he envisioned his fists clutched around two hairy throats his fingers flexed, his jaw clenched, and his eyes smoldered with grim anticipation.

Footsteps approached from behind, carrying the scent of new-washed hair as if on a summer breeze. A hand touched his shoulder, and the suddenly decapitated heads of imagined wolves leaped into the air on geysers of blood. One of Haldred's waifs cleared her throat.

"More mead?" she said.

"Aye," he answered, his voice like the ghost of an earthquake.

Her thin arms lifted the great oaken bowl, and as her footsteps receded, he gazed at the fire, and his fists and jaw slowly unclenched.

Melwyn, he thought to himself, *her name is Melwyn.*

"Melwyn!"

The shout tore Thurnglad's gaze from the fire. He turned to see Mordall clutching Melwyn's arm, causing her to drop Thurnglad's bowl. Mordall was a warrior, one of the best, but the loudest of the braggarts. "Doff thine apron and dance with me!"

"I'd sooner go a'reeling with a trout," said Melwyn, bracing her feet against the tug of his brawn. The hall fell silent. Even through the back of Mordall's head Thurnglad could see his darting eyes. In a moment the churl would find an insult to hurl before stepping away. Thurnglad had seen it before.

This time, however, Mordall leaned back and wrenched her arm in the direction of the dancers. "I *asked* you to dance," he snarled.

Thurnglad arose, inhaling fury, but before his ire could be expelled, Melwyn drew a dagger from behind her apron and slashed at Mordall's arm. She wounded only his leathern sleeve, but he leaped back, staring at her in disbelief.

"You filthy fish!" he said in his meanest, most petulant voice, a tone he normally reserved for those few (Thurnglad included) who bested him in sparring. He reached for his own dagger, but stopped when he noticed Thurnglad striding toward him.

Thurnglad took no notice now of Mordall's shifting eyes. His only thought was to grip and squeeze until eyes burst from sockets. He lunged forward, then pulled up short when Melwyn stepped in front of him.

"Your mead is coming, sir," she said. "Kindly beseat yourself."

Thurnglad blinked, amazed that she would so blithely turn her back on her foe, but Mordall was at a loss himself. For a moment, Thurnglad studied her eyes, and was daunted by the fire he saw there. Confused, he stepped back. Where had she gotten such courage? He had never before seen it in her. Sparing one more glance at Mordall, he shook his head and returned to his seat.

A bellowing laugh erupted from Mordall. "She put you in your place, eh, oxwife?" For the space of a breath the hush in the mead hall deepened, then, like an ice-locked river breaking apart in the spring, the hall erupted with the clatter of cutlery and the scraping of benches as everyone rushed for the walls. In Thurnglad's head, the sound was like a great bear roaring the word that in human speech is rendered "Death!" Without turning around, Thurnglad took three deep breaths, until it seemed to him that he grew to twice his normal size. He turned around. Melwyn was still there, hands on her hips, her back to Mordall. The only way to put an end to Mordall's chuckling was to go through her, and yet she too seemed to have grown, effectively eclipsing his foe. Like a bear assailed by a swarm of bees, he lowered his head and stumbled toward the door.

Outside, alone with his rage and confusion, he wanted to bellow, to rip up trees by their roots. He wanted to go back inside and kill everyone there. He walked a few paces into the eerily glowing snow and focused on breathing evenly the thin frozen air. Slowly the smell of pine trees and cowsheds quieted his roiling emotions, and he stood for several minutes like a tree that waits for spring.

The door opened behind him. Footsteps crunched through the snow. He smelled mead and new-washed hair. He turned around.

Melwyn was lifting a bowl of mead to him, her arms trembling from the weight and the cold.

"Here," she said. Pent-up breath streamed from her mouth as he took the bowl from her. For a moment they stared at each other, then Melwyn smiled and hugged herself. "Cold," she said. She started to turn, then hesitated, took a breath, and held it. Suddenly she laughed, as if at her own confusion, and trotted back inside.

Thurnglad stared after her, then slowly turned his back once more to the meadhall and stared out over the valley. He nodded, as if he understood something, then hefted the bowl to his lips. Long moments passed while the mead coursed down his throat. When the vessel was empty, he let out his breath with a gasp.

He cast the bowl aside and walked into the woods to relieve himself. By the time he stepped out from the trees, his mind was singing with the strength of the mead, and his stride was wavering pleasantly. He picked up the meadbowl, to bring it back inside, then remembered Mordall, and suddenly he wanted to uproot trees again. He resolved to put Mordall in his place, then thought of Melwyn, and his confusion returned. He stood transfixed, held taut by conflicting desires, flexing his fingers against the bowl's wooden resilience.

His anger swelled until he could no longer contain it, and he started to run. Below him lay the steep ravine that had been cleared of trees generations ago so that no enemy could take them by surprise. Holding the bowl before him he leaped over the edge. For a moment, such was the strength of his leap, he thought he might not come down, but would fly into the night like an owl. Suddenly, his anger dropped from him and bounced down the ravine, shattering as it fell. His eyes widened as he realized he was about to follow it. Clutching the bowl to his chest, he prayed, confessing all his sins since boyhood, and asked for a miracle.

The hard-packed, icy snow crunched under the impact, and then he was hurtling downhill, racing along on top of the bowl, bits of snow stinging his face and the wind pulling at his hair. Bumps and hillocks tossed him in the air, and the glowing snow and the sentinel trees raced past and underneath him until he was terrified and overwhelmed with joy. When he reached the bottom he slid for a quarter of a mile, spinning slowly until the stillness enshrouded him, and for a moment he made no move, his legs suspended above the snow. Then a grin slashed his lips, fierce behind his ice-flecked beard. He jumped to his feet and ran back up the mountain.

By morning he had made a dozen runs and was nearly exhausted. The clouds had retreated, as if the stars had pushed them aside to watch, but the only indication that morning had arrived was the lowing of the cattle. When he reached the top once more, a small boy was there, bundled in sheep skin, eyes wide with wonder. Without a word the boy lifted his arms and Thurnglad's smile faltered. He was suddenly aware of tiny faces at the doors of a dozen huts. He swallowed and squared his shoulders.

Walking past the boy, he carried the bowl to the tanner's shed, where he nailed a leather strap slack across the top of the bowl. He considered waiting there until the children lost interest, but his chest was still full of the exhilaration of descent, so he drew a deep breath, released it, and forced himself to face them.

He carried the modified bowl to the slope and placed it next to the boy. He settled himself in crosslegged, and pulled the strap up over his knees. Without invitation, the boy climbed into his lap and set his face toward the valley. Thurnglad tugged on the strap to inch them over the lip of the slope and waited for the boy to scream. It never happened. The ride was as wild as any of them, but the boy sat delighted between his knees and faced the descent without flinching. *A warrior born,* he thought, and was proud of his village. He carried the boy back up on his shoulders, and was greeted at the top by every child in the village, clamoring for a turn.

He pointed sternly to two, and gathered them into his lap. They screamed all the way down, and never had any sound pleased him more. The three of them ran back up the hill and he took two more down with him. Not only children were gathering at the top of the slope, but maids, matrons and crones, warriors, fathers and grandfathers had arrived to watch with puzzled smiles. He spent the whole day giving rides to children and spending his strength as he had never done in any battle, real or imagined.

He saw Mordall at the edge of the crowd, bereft of his usual leer. In the spirit of his newfound exuberance he allowed himself to shout "Grab a meadbowl, Mordall!" before hurtling downhill. On his way back up, Mordall sped past him, headfirst like a black otter, with a child riding his back. Thurnglad shook his head in wonder, and would have stopped, but one of the children with him grabbed his hand and urged him to hurry.

Melwyn was there as well, leading a few of the shyer children toward him by the hand. Only once did he catch her eye as she placed a child in his lap. The levelness of her gaze unnerved him, and when she gave him a push he was almost killed, and the children with him, for the warm impression of her hands on his back so stirred his heart that he had trouble staying balanced.

By late afternoon, when the grayness was deepening once more into black, every able body in the village was hurtling down the mountain on meadbowls and serving trays and anything else that would slide. When at last Thurnglad collapsed on his back, too tired to walk up the hill, the two children with him pulled at him, imploring him to continue the game, but he was spent, his chest heaving like a blacksmith's bellows, with nothing but the joy in his heart to keep him conscious.

Dimly he heard a commotion, and within minutes he was aswarm with children, all pulling and laughing. By some miracle of communal strength they dragged him all the way up the mountain. By the time they reached the top he had regained enough of his breath to let out a roar of triumph into the black and glittering sky. The entire village bellowed back at him, and it was as if the sun had returned, and the ice and the darkness, for all their boastings, had no strength to beat back its rays.

The Frog Who Was Not Quite a Prince

(2011)

Once upon a time, there was a beautiful princess who was truly evil. All right, she wasn't really a princess, but she was quite sure she ought to be. Her name was Thanatea, and she considered that perhaps she had been adopted. Yes, her mother had the same silky blonde hair as her and her father the same delicate ears, but she thought, somewhat confusedly, that maybe they had been adopted themselves, or perhaps her great-grandparents had once been royalty before being wickedly deposed in a popular uprising.

She made many attempts to demonstrate her princessness. An early scheme had involved sneaking peas from her dinner plate to shove beneath her mattress, but after five minutes of violent tossings and turnings she had fallen asleep exhausted only to awake up the next morning refreshed and well-rested. Another plan had involved spreading rumors about a curse and stealing a bottle of sleeping pills from the medicine cabinet. Fortunately for her, the rumor reached her mother, and her plan (and the pills) were discovered before she could set the scheme in motion. Undeterred, she watched every Disney princess movie she could find and had her parents read her all the princess-related fairy tales they could find, but it seemed as though every princess in cognito had to undure hardships with long-suffering patience until someone eventually arrived to reveal their princessity.

Which seemed like far too much trouble, so she turned to magic. Never mind where she found the books, nor what she did to procure them (trust me—you really don't want to know). She mastered love potions quickly, but she could only test them on regular boys on behalf of regular girls, since there were so few princes in the area. None at all, in fact, which is why—though she had avoided this option as long as possible—she at last resorted to frog kissing.

First she developed a magical test to determine whether a frog was really a prince, and then she set about capturing and testing frogs. In truth, the magic was rather simple—she administered a dose of poisoned pocket-lint orally to each frog and waited to see which one survived. As luck would have it, it took less than fifty tries to find one that passed the test. The frog was little and not particularly ugly, but she could not suppress a shudder as she brought it to her mouth. She made sure her kiss was a good one, soft and lingering, so she wouldn't have to administer it twice, but nothing happened. She observed him carefully for several minutes, but he showed no sign of growing or changing into anything. Disappointed, she tossed him back into the pond.

Poor frog. His great-great-great-great-great-great-great-grandfather had been an evil prince, transformed by a spell that had backfired to the great relief of the people over which he would otherwise eventually have ruled. This little frog knew nothing of that, yet constantly he yearned for a smaller pond.

Alas, with that one, gentle kiss he fell instantly, hopelessly in love.

He clambered out of the pond and followed the evil princess everywhere. Thanatea, however, took no further notice of him. Having judged her frog experiments a failure, she moved on to other endeavors, and so frogs, like most anything else for which she had no use, became invisible to her. Which was just as well, since otherwise, she might have kicked, stomped upon or otherwise abused and ultimately killed him. The frog did not go out of his way to draw attention to himself but was content merely to stare openmouthed at the object of his great affection.

He took little notice of her activities, and so was largely ignorant of her wickedness. At those odd times when he couldn't help but be shocked by her cruelty (such as when she swatted flies and let them drop, lifeless and uneaten, to the floor) he simply explained to himself that he was only a little frog in a big, big world, and he couldn't be expected to know how other beings measured good and evil.

In time the evil princess hit upon a brilliant idea: Rather than striving endlessly (and thus far fruitlessly) to prove her princessitude, she need only start acting the part. For that she required a lady-in-waiting, so she sought out and found a littler girl who adored her and was willing to be bullied and bossed around. She didn't bother asking her name, which was Zoetrope.

Is it necessary even to mention that the little frog was made greener still by envy? He would have given anything to be bossed around and bullied by the one who had once smacked him so deliciously on the lips.

Coincidentally, Zoetrope's great-great-grandmother had been a princess in Sweden before she'd been turned into a bear. Part of that story may be found elsewhere (specifically the part where the curse was eventually lifted), but the descendants of this bear princess had fallen onto hard times had forgotten their former royal ursinity. The little girl was not beautiful, if only because no one had ever told her she was.

One day, when Thanatea was casting about for some new cruel command she could inflict upon her maid-servant, her attention turned at last to the love-struck frog. Needless to say she didn't recognize him, but only saw a fresh chance to humiliate her single subject. She lifted the frog (who was instantly transported with bliss), told her he was really a handsome prince, and ordered the littler girl to kiss him. Zoetrope recoiled in disgust but, having maintained her naïveté in spite of Thanatea's past manipulations, overcame her revulsion, closed her eyes, puckered her lips, and leaned forward.

The frog would have leapt away in equal disgust had not Thanatea's grip been so strong. She smooshed the frog's face hard into Zoetrope's lips, then suddenly dropped him as though she had received an electrical shock.

The little frog knew nothing of electricity, but he knew that he wasn't feeling well. Revolted as he was by the kiss and stunned as he was by the two-foot drop to the ground, his agony was greater than either cause could account for. He writhed and contorted pitiably as his limbs ached and swelled, and he hardly noticed the little girls growing a little less little.

Zoetrope shrieked, but the evil princess only stared at her with dull hatred. The cause of the frog's distress was obvious: Being a true princess, she had succeeded in transforming him into a prince.

Well, almost.

It had been many generations since the evil prince had turned himself into a frog, and his hapless descendants were now mostly only frog, so now he was transforming into a grotesque, human-like frog-creature about the size of a toddler. The evil princess felt vindicated: "Aha!" she cried, "Not so much of a princess, I guess!" But the true princess, recovering somewhat from her initial shock, felt intense compassion for the monster. "Help!" she cried.

The frog-prince was in unendurable pain. He breathed in short, spasmodic gasps, gulping air as though the planet were running low. He could say only one human word, but he repeated it over and over:

"Ow. Ow. Ow. Ow. Ow. Ow."

The true princess fell to the ground and embraced him, smothering the creature with kisses, but they made no difference. Her tears fell upon his hideous cheeks to no avail.

So sharp and poignant were the true princess's emotions that the evil princess herself began to feel distress. She hated the stabs of empathy, as she hated everything and wanted nothing more than to make them stop, so, without pausing to consider, she pried the littler girl away from the hideous frog-thing and kissed him herself.

Immediately he was transformed back into a green little traumatized frog.

"You saved him!" Zoetrope cried and threw her arms tight around Thanatea's neck. So relieved and grateful was she that she kissed the evil princess on the lips. Thanatea staggered backwards, terrified of the power in her lady-in-waiting's kiss, but she did not appear to be transforming, and so she attempted to cover her panic with a sneer. "Besmirch not our royal lips with thy froggy ones," she said, imperiously.

Nevertheless, there was indeed power in Zoetrope's kiss. Though neither was aware of it at the time, she had inadvertantly transformed her bossy playmate into a princess good and true.

During the rest of that long, hot summer, they had many adventures, and for the rest of their lives they were always close friends. The little frog was kept by his true love in a glass terrarium in her room, and she never failed to provide him with food, fresh water and (what he craved the most) attention, and they all lived happily ever after.

The End.

Go to Hell

(1989)

Johnny floored the accelerator of his '77 Monte Carlo 350 and left a pair of thirty foot black pythons smoldering on the Tennessee pavement. Everyone in the neighborhood either shook their heads or smiled, depending on how old they were. Johnny let out a rebel yell and downshifted, just to hear the engine yell back. He pushed Aerosmith into the cassette player and cranked the volume. He sped through a red light and laughed at the dwindling blare of old men leaning on horns and shaking their fists.

He hung a left on Maple Ave. and let the back end fishtail to within a yard of old Mrs. Marpleson's snot-black terrier. Christ, he'd like to ram that mutt up Marpleson's ass. He saw Dean's house up on the right and stood on the brakes as he whaled on the steering wheel. "Das Boot" swung an abrupt about-face and slammed into the sidewalk on the other side of the road. He straight-armed the horn until Dean leaped out the door, one arm in his denim jacket, the other clutching a six of Bud.

"Haul ass, man! My dad's on a fuckin' rampage," yelled Dean, falling into the seat.

Johnny swiveled his eyes back at the house, and saw Mr. Daniels running out the door with a face that would've made Beelzebub cringe. Mr. Daniels' mind was ablaze with a fiery red rage. He meant to give Johnny a piece of his mind, and maybe a bite of his fist. Johnny let him plant one foot on the pavement, then floored it and flipped him the bird as he squealed away. "Fuckerrr!" Johnny screamed. "Toss me a Bud." Mr. Daniels raced after them, banging his hand on the trunk and screaming and squealing until he ran out of breath, and stopped in the middle of the street, leaning his hands on his knees and gasping like a vacuum cleaner on the fritz.

Dean ripped a can out of the six-pack and said, "Jesus Fucking Christ, man, he's gonna fucking kill me. He's gonna fucking flush me down the fucking toilet, man."

"Fuck him," said Johnny serenely, and downshifted again, just to hear the engine yell.

"Man, he's gonna fucking kill me," said Dean, his voice raspy from repetition and the smoke from his Camels. "He's gonna fucking can my ass." They were sitting on the Monte Carlo's hood, looking out at Palumpset Pond. Dean imagined his father cuffing him into the wall, bringing chunks of plaster down from the ceiling.

"Big fucking deal, so he kills you, so what? Shut up about it already, Christ." Johnny took another pull of 151 gin and shoved the bottle into Dean's chest. "Quit bawling and drink."

Dean tipped the bottle back, and handed it back to Johnny.

"You call that a drink, ya fucking pussy? Pull on it. Go on: pull!"

Dean pulled and rested the bottle on his knee. "He's gonna kill me, man. Fucking kill me." He was kicking at the fender like a restless little kid. Christ, his dad was really going to kill him.

Johnny stood up and pulled off his shirt. He had a lean, muscular chest with hair down to his belly button. A pair of dog tags jangled between his nipples. "C'mon. We're going swimming."

"It's fucking October, Johnny, I ain't swimming in fucking October." Dean hated to whine, but Christ, why'd Johnny want to go swimming in fucking October?

Johnny swiveled his eyes towards Dean and slowly thrust out his jaw. "I don't care if it's fucking Christmas. I said we're swimming—so strip."

Dean turned and looked intently, though blankly, toward the left-hand shore of the pond, blinking his eyes and mouth. "Oh, man, I don't believe this shit." The pond was like a big mirror, and Dean had always been afraid of mirrors, especially after his father had shoved his head through one when he was six. He slumped off the hood and shook off his denim jacket, then slowly peeled off his black tank top. His chest was sunken and bony, and there was a tiny heart tatooed on his solar plexus.

Johnny was already down to his boxers and loping off to the edge of the water. Dean groaned and dropped his chinos and trotted after him, positive he was going to catch double pneumonia. "Fucking A, man," he moaned, watching Johnny bull through the water at a full gallop and dive in. He came up puffing like an ox, and turned to watch Dean.

Dean danced through the water like a fucking girl, straining the cords of his neck, then floundered when he ran too deep. Christ, sometimes the guy could be a fucking wuss. He was OK when he wasn't whining about his father, but Christ, you'd think his father was some demon from hell the way he acted sometimes. Christ. Johnny crested backwards into the water and roared, just to hear the echo roar back. Christ it was cold.

A duck flew overhead and quacked. It took one look at the two humans and decided to find some other pond to sit in. *Fucking humans are taking over the world*, it thought.

Dean stood up, spluttering and staggering like he was having an epileptic siezure and a heart attack at the same time. Christ, he was fucking dying. It was *that* fucking cold.

Johnny laughed as loudly as he could, just to hear the echo laugh back.

Sheriff Donovan just loved to catch young boys with their pants down. And these boys had left their trousers on the beach. "You boys having a good time out there?" he called, pleased with the congenial threat in his voice.

Dean dove under water as if he could stay there for a week. Sheriff Donovan was a mean son of a bitch. He and his father were good friends. He was dead for sure.

Johnny stopped swimming and treaded water, calm as before a storm. "Afternoon, sheriff." Smelly fart son of a bitch. "What's on your mind?"

"Well now, I been getting a few phone calls down to the station. Seems a couple of young ruffians been tearing through town in a big blue automobile whose description pretty well matches this here behemoth I'm leaning on. Either of you boys know anything about a couple of young ruffians?"

Dean's head popped to the surface facing the wrong direction. "Is he gone yet?"

Johnny ignored him and said, "Can't say that I do, sheriff."

"How about you, Deanny? You know anything about some young ruffians tearing about this fair principality of ours?" He paused to listen to Dean splutter, then said, "I kinda considered you didn't." He paused again, just to let the tension build, then picked up the bottle of 151 off the hood of the car. "Well now. Well now, it occurs to me that this here's what we call an open container. Now, if my memory serves me correctly, this here's town property I'm standing on. It further occurs to me that open containers and town property don't mix, wouldn't you agree, Mr. Johnson?" *Shit, this is fun,* he thought. "Well? Answer me, boy. Devil got your tongue, or what? Ha ha ha!

Johnny needed time to think, and old Ironsides there wasn't going to give him any, so he reached over and grabbed Dean by the hair on the back of his neck and plunged him face first into the water. While Dean struggled, Johnny commenced to think. It wasn't easy. His mind seemed funny, somehow, like it wasn't entirely his own. He tensed up his brows and concentrated as hard as he could on how he was going to get out of this scrape. Really, it was amazing how ineffectual Dean's struggling was.

Dean struggled ineffectually. He writhed and squirmed and finally screamed. At the end of his scream he found he had no choice but to inhale pondwater. Immediately his lungs seemed to rupture and although his eyes were wide, the greenish pondlight began to darken and fade. *I'm dying,* he thought: *my father's gonna fucking kill me.*

Remarkably, he still found strength to struggle. He thrashed; he screamed; he drew more water into his lungs. The grip on his hair tightened and he was pulled up. When the pulling stopped, he was standing, and the water came up only to his knees. He looked around and was completely blown away by the scenery. He started to say something to Johnny, but found that Johnny wasn't there. Instead, it was the Night Stalker that had Dean's neck in a vise-like grip.

The Californian serial killer smiled and said, "Welcome to Disneyland."

Dean's eyes widened as he looked around and around and around like an owl on acid. Apparently, he was in the lake that contained the submarine from 20,000 Leagues Under the Sea. Apparently, he was, indeed, in Disneyland. "Does this mean I'm dead?" he asked.

In the distance, he could hear Goofy laughing demoniacally.

The Night Stalker let go of his neck and walked away towards Space Mountain. Dean continued goggling like a land-locked, big-mouthed, yellow-bellied, cantankerous, jelly-bellied, weak-kneed, puling, sniffling, sneezing, coughing, aching, stuffy-head, fever-so-you-can-rest (what was I going to say? Ah yes.) ... blowfish. Dean continued to look like this until he noticed someone else he recognized.

It was Julie McCoy, the cruise director from "The Love Boat." Behind her were Captain Steubing, Gopher, and Isaac. The other cast members had presumably gone on to bigger and better things. "Welcome to Hell," said Julie, brightly. "If you'll please join the rest of the group, we'll continue the Grand Tour."

"The rest of the group" consisted of a crowd that could have filled the Astrodome like grain in a silo. In other words, not using the seats, but piled on top of each other like fish in a trawler. That is, packed in in such a way that they'd have to be dropped in through a small hole in the top of the dome until it was full, and you'd have to use a jackhammer on the bodies on top in order to squeeze them all in. Do you get the picture?

Obviously, there were very few people Dean recognized in the crowd. Most were Ethiopians, judging from the distended bellies and sunken chests. Others looked Arabian. One person he did recognize was Bette

Davis, who was waving a long cigarette and talking garrulously with an old man Dean didn't recognize, who had a large pocketwatch draped on his head like pizza dough. To avoid any confusion, you should know that this man was Salvador Dali, the surrealist painter that had died earlier in the year. He did not like being talked to by Bette Davis, but what could he do? He was in Hell.

Dean joined the group, and tried to listen to what Julie McCoy was saying.

"Now on the left is Wonderland, home of Alice and all her zany friends."

Dean had no idea who Alice was, but he didn't like the look of the dragon thing that was whiffling through the tulgy wood. A few yards away from Dean, Mel Blanc was being accosted by a faceless grin. "C'mon," it was purring, "Do Sylvester for me, huh? How about Porky Pig? I always liked Porky Pig. Do Foghorn, huh? C'mon, I'm a big fan of yours, what do you say?"

"Fuck off," said Mel, swinging an axe.

Julie McCoy said, "And over here is Jungleland with Mowglie and all his zany friends.

Mowglie was hunched on an earthenware pot with his hands over his ears, wearing a look of intense perturbation. He was glaring at a huge video screen which pictured Axl Rose screaming, "Welcome to the Jungle." Dean's spirit picked up at once, and he started air guitaring until Jimmy Paige walked up to him and said, "It gets pretty annoying after a while, actually." Jimmy looked as if he'd been there for quite a while.

Julie Mccoy said, "and over here is Graceland, with . . . is that Humpty Dumpty on the wall?" A spotlight illuminated a dumpy figure with a white cravat wielding a microphone. "Why, it's Elvis, ladies and gentlemen," chimed Julie McCoy. "Let's give a big hand for the king of Rock and Roll. Yayyyyy!"

Scattered applause rippled through the vast crowd as Elvis cleared his throat with a sound like a cat being dragged over hot coals by its tail. He waited for the feedback to whine away, thrust his pelvis toward the crowd, fastened one hand to his grease-laden hair and crooned, "A one for the money, two for the show, three -"

He was interrupted by a monstrous explosion of bilious, sulfurous, cloying smog through which I stepped forth and commanded, "Stop that! If I've told you a billion times, I've told you a googolplex of times, never, never, *never* sing. Off to the tar pits with you, until I can think of a more suitable torment." Elvis had time to twang out, "Aw, shit," before I sent him, with a wave of my hand, to a night club, where he was scheduled to compete in an Elvis impersonation contest. Damn my mind works fast!

"All right," I boomed, as satanically as I could, "break it up, go on, there's nothing to see here, move along, YOU! is that a beer I see in your hand?" I pointed to Dean, just because he was so pathetic, and conjured a cup of beer into his hand.

"Shit!" yelled Dean, as he dropped the cup.

"Aha!" I roared. "Littering! Misdemeanor! Up against the wall, maggot! Ha ha ha ha haaaa!" I handcuffed him and threw him to the ground, then disappeared.

A young man named Walt stood over Dean and said, "Big deal. You should have gone to college in New Hampshire. That was frightening." He kicked Dean in the kidney and walked away. I made a note to hire Walt after he'd been around a few millenia.

Sheriff Donovan pulled out his gun with something approaching ecstacy. He had never shot a man in his life, and here was Johnny Johnson, in the midst of murdering Dean Daniels. The Colt .44 was gonna leave a hole the size of the state in Johnny's head, and he would be hailed as a hero for it. Applause drifted faintly to his ear as if from a seashell, as he steadied the sight on Johnny's nose. Screams of adoration made his ears ring as he gently, lovingly, squeezed the trigger. His hand was all tingly, and his ears hurt as he watched Johnny slowly sink into the pond, a portion of his skull missing, his head looking like a crescent moon. The echo of the gunshot roared back at him, and he smiled so widely that his dentures came loose.

The Wicked Witch of the East descended on Dean and ripped the handcuffs off, severing both hands at the wrist. Dean gaped at the stumps while the Wicked Witch cackled, until blood erupted into his face. A small audience gathered to laugh at him, but quickly got bored and wandered off. "Your friend just died," wheedled the witch.

Dean was silent for what seemed like twenty years while he tried to remember what a friend was and what it might look like. "Johnny?" he said at last. "Johnny's dead? Can I see him?"

The Wicked Witch cackled hideously, though perhaps not with as much vigour as she had fifty years ago, and said, "Not in this eternity, Boy Blunder." She cackled some more until a monkey came to fly her away. Dean shook his head in wonder. "So Johnny made it to heaven," he said, sadly. His hands crawled up his pantlegs and dropped themselves into his pockets. He disliked the way they fidgeted and fingered his loose change.

Something tugged at the back of his shirt and he turned around. As he did so, his head fell off for no apparent reason and landed face down in the pool of blood left by his hands. His body shrugged its shoulders and kicked Dean's head down the road. A Cheshire smile appeared above the gaping neck as his body ran after its head. A bunch of people saw this and picked teams for a soccer game. The game was in full swing, with the team with flayed skin beginning to edge out the team with mutilated body parts, when Dean's head managed to get hold of a flayed foot with his teeth and refused to let go. Someone suggested that they cut off the foot, but someone else pointed out that the head wouldn't roll as well with a foot in its mouth. Since the person who had pointed this out was Einstein, they decided he was probably right and all wandered away, leaving Dean with his victim, who was trying to gnaw at Dean's head. Three centuries passed before Dean's father happened to walk by. Dean's jaw dropped and the person with flayed skin scurried away. Dean slammed his eyes shut and bolted them, and pulled a bureau and a few chairs in back of them and hoped that his father wouldn't see him.

Dean's father picked up the head and held it by the forehead and back of the head, which felt strange since most of the hair had been pulled out by the man with flayed skin and his scalp was horribly gouged. For a moment, the man caressed his son's head reflectively and smoothed the sparse hair. He seemed to remember the short time he had spent with his son on earth. He smiled tenderly, his eyes lost in the red glare of the infernal horizon. "Ah, hell," he said, and with perfect, Doug Flutey form, he kicked his son in the ear with the laces of his shoes and sent him howling silently over the horizon. Then he grinned such a huge grin that the corners of his mouth met at the rear and the top of his head fell off. He took some Krazy Glue™ out of his pocket and smeared an even layer on both of the surfaces he wanted to join, and wandered off with the top of his head glued to the side of his ass. The only thing the bottom of his head was good for was eating cereal out of (asshole!).

"Eeeyyyhhhh," said Bugs Bunny slowly, taking a bite out of his carrot and chewing it a few times before swallowing, "What's up, Doc?"

Dean tried to follow the cartoon character with his eyes, but as his head was spinning as it flew, he kept losing sight of his gray and white companion with the Brooklyn accent.

"Pardon me," said the little bunny rabbit with the powder puff tail, "but are you aware of the factual conundrium that you are presently in, namely that you're headed straight for—" and here the crazy varmint paused for effect, and to draw a big breath, before opening his mouth to roughly the size of the Lincoln Tunnel and screaming,

before putting one hand on the top of his head and the other on the bottom of his feet, and squeezing himself out of existence.

A moment later, the back of Dean's head collided with something hard. He bounced to the ground face up and stared into a strangely familiar face. "Oh, wise guy, huh?" said Curly, before taking a double take at Dean's severed head and saying, "Wa-a-a!" and running panicked into Moe, who said, "Watch it, ya big lump," and tweaked Curly's nose. Then he saw Dean, and yelled, and both of them ran into Larry, who was looking in the other direction. Larry turned and started to say something, then saw Dean, opened his eyes really wide and said, "Hey, wait for me!" and ran after Moe and Curly until they were all out of sight. They did that a lot in Hell.

"Ah say, Ah say, what's the hurry, boys?" asked Foghorn Leghorn of the three receding forms. "Damn kids, Ah say, what's this here we have here? The Easter Bunny leave you behind, there, son? Now don't lose your head now, haw, haw, haw."

"Fuck off," Dean muttered.

"Don't mind if I do," said Foghorn, leering at Mother Goose. "Excuse me, Madam," he said, taking her arm and leading her away.

Dean wondered if, being in Cartoon Hell, someone might be able to draw some sort of body for him. He was tired of being kicked around.

Perhaps you are wondering what was happening in Nazi Germany at that moment. Hitler had just delivered his famous speech at Heidelburg, and was taking a nice hot bath with Eva Braun, when it suddenly occured to him that he was not wearing any clothes. He jumped out of the tub and hastily wrapped a towel around himself, his face flushed with rage and shame. After casting a look of indignant fury at Eva, he goose stepped out of the bathroom, leaving strict orders for a storm trooper to stand eternal guard at the door, armed with a flaming sword. A little while later, I'm afraid he went a little mad.

Now, in every person's life, there comes a time of choice.

Johnny Johnson squinted his eyes at the rows upon rows of shelves upon shelves of eyeballs upon eyeballs, and wondered if he might not have found a better pair. He wondered if he might not have been better off choosing some bigger ones, or perhaps a couple with a slightly paler shade of green. But the fussy old angel had insisted that he not try on different pairs. *Unsanitary,* she had said. *This isn't Filene's basement.* So Johnny would just have to like it or lump it. At least he had gotten a good nose.

He wandered out of the eyeball warehouse, and stopped a passing cherub to ask directions to the finger factory. He had found some really nice, long fingers, the kind with self-cleaning nails, but he had belatedly noticed that the ring finger on the right hand was longer than the middle one. He was damned if he wasn't going to demand that they give him an exchange. It never occured to him that he might have put them on wrong.

Seventeen trillion billion years passed, give or take a millenium, and Dean had seen just about all the sights that hell had to offer. He had indeed been given a cartoon body, but as it could not support his head, he had had to have that drawn, too. He looked like an odd cross between Goofy and Winnie-the-Pooh. He was long and angular, but there was something about his eye and smile that suggested a slightly manic version of Pooh. He was often heard to hum snatches of nonsense, like, "Tra-la-la, tra-la-la, tra-la-la, tra-la-la, rum-tum-tum-tiddle-um," in a voice that was not quite his own.

Every once in a while he would come across his headless body wandering through the steamier sections of hell, walking with a peculiar jaunt in its step which Dean could not remember ever having. Occasionally, he would see some Italians playing soccer and notice they were using his head, which had begun to look rather worn.

A sadness overtook him one—I almost said day, but there was no such thing—that was deeper than any emotion he had ever previously experienced. Around him, people were laughing and drinking, and seeming to have the same good times they had had while alive. The old baseball players had even gotten a bunch of teams together and were playing an exhibition game in a field across from where he was standing. He had always heard that hell was all eternal flame and heat and torture, but here he was, not even perspiring. Yet he felt an emptiness that was profound. He was alone. Hell needed none of its traditional horrors to draw out the horrors of his miserable existence. He shoved his cartoon hands into his cartoon pockets and stood where he was, chin clenched to chest, for the next 4.6 billion years.

When he looked up, he saw a batter swing and, a second later, the crack of ball hitting bat reached his stubby ears. He couldn't be sure, but it seemed as if he had seen that very same pitcher winding up for the very same batter those few billions of years earlier. It was as if the time hadn't passed at all, and yet, whole worlds had been born in his mind during that time, stars had formed and collapsed, galaxies had spun themselves into oblivion. For the final 10,000 years, he had focused his thoughts solely on the inhabitants of a single planet. He couldn't lose the feeling that something vaguely important had happened during that time, but he couldn't put his cartoon finger on exactly what it was. He shrugged his lanky shoulders and walked towards the game, thinking he'd buy a hot dog, or something.

As he walked, a heavy fog enveloped him, thick with voices. He looked around, slowly: he could see nothing except the dense white cloud he had somehow wandered into. The voices sounded hollow and sinister, as if they were being spoken into a giant tin can. He couldn't see his feet. The mist seemed to be making the ink in his cartoon body run and fade; he was discorporating completely!

Is this the end of Dean Daniels? Is he acually going to fade away into oblivion, this close to existential fulfillment?

Well, yes, I mean, what's the point? Fulfillment isn't allowed in hell.

Johnny had lost his mind. Not his brain, which was still as warm and pink as the day he had first gotten in line for it, but that part of his brain which had been responsible for keeping organized the reasoning centers of the cerebellum had simply shut down under the pressure of so many contradictions. Johnny just couldn't understand the people in heaven. So goddamned serene, always singing, always making a great show of loving each other as if all of heaven were some platonic, bisexual orgy, or something. It was enough to drive one crazy.

He was wandering around in some clouds one day, constantly fiddling with his halo like a dog worrying a collar, when he happened to notice a shimmer, a wavering in the air like a heat mirage. He flew over to it with his huge, ungainly wings and caught hold of it with his gown and wrapped it up securely. He glanced about furtively, and tried to act as if the rather large bulge in the folds of his cloak might be no more than a tumor of some sort. Uncomfortable with this, he crossed the tips of his wings over the protuberance, like someone caught naked in a public place. He wanted to take it to a cave somewhere and brood over the treasure, but there was no privacy to speak of in heaven: only the spare moment caught in the open sky when no one happened to be looking. Or at least, no one seemed to be looking.

"Johnny?"

Johnny squinted his eyes and looked around suspiciously. This wasn't the first time he had heard voices.

"Johnny? It's me, let me out."

Johnny rolled his eyes and twitched, as if he had cerebral palsy. He seemed to be trying to follow thoughts that were playing children's games like Hide-and-Go-Seek and Ring-Around-the-Rosy. Finally he looked down at his treasure.

"It's me: Dean. Is that you, Johnny? Let me out, OK? Where am I, anyway?"

Johnny carefully lifted a corner of his robe, keeping his face as far away as possible and grimacing, as if he expected a swarm of bees to fly out.

Instead, the vague shimmer leaked out and hovered in front of him, looking vaguely familiar. Screwing his eyes up and tilting his head, Johnny could just make out… No, he thought it was Goofy, but… It almost looked like Winnie-the-Pooh, but…

"It's me, Dean Daniels. Don't you remember? You killed me."

Johnny looked up sharply, an old flame glowing in his new eyes. "Dean," he said, nodding his head like a pigeon. "Johnny remembers Dean. Yeah. Yeah. But Johnny didn't kill Dean. No sir. Dean's father must have killed Dean. Elsewise, why would Johnny be *here*? Eh?"

He looked up at Dean sharply and shrewdly, the tatters of his sanity hanging from his shoulders and draped over his wings.

"And if you're Dean," he continued, without changing his expression, "then how come you got a little powder puff tail?"

Dean started and strained to see his rear end. "I don't see no—any powder puff tail."

"Oh," said Johnny, taking a Fifth Avenue candy bar out of the breast pocket of his robe and taking a bite out of the wrapper. He seemed suddenly unaware of Dean's presence.

Dean stood (or floated) a while in thought. After a week or two, he looked up at Johnny, who was still chewing on the candy wrapper and looking oblivious. He shrugged his shoulders and let himself drift upwards. He waited for Johnny to call out, or chase after him, but nothing of the sort was forthcoming.

He floated upwards for six days before seeing anyone else. On the seventh day, he was accosted by a strange creature with a dozen or so dove's wings revolving around a dozen or so eyes. With no apparent mouth to speak from, the creature nonetheless addressed him, saying, "Come on, hurry up, you're late, do you realize that your planet was consumed by the sun three and a half eons ago? Where have you been?"

Dean thought it best not to answer, and was relieved when the creature said, "Never mind, come along to the warehouses with me. There's not a lot left to choose from, I'm afraid, but it's all quality stuff, so not to worry. Hurry up—it's almost over, for Christ's sake."

Dean looked down through the depths of blue and white, hoping to catch a glimpse of Johnny, but the air was empty. He gave the slightest ethereal shrug and followed the creature ever upwards.

When at last they arrived at the gates of heaven, after six more days, St. Peter jumped up from his booth and rushed them inside. "My God, man, what's kept you? We're almost ready. Come, I'll take you to the warehouse, myself. You do have your papers, don't you? Ah well, it can't be helped. Not much point in it, anyway, I'd say. Hurry along, now."

The warehouses were great, golden buildings with ornate doors the size of middle class houses. St. Peter led him to the side of one of the doors and opened it just enough to let them pass through.

"Luckily, we consolidated all of the body parts once the earth was consumed. To tell the truth, we weren't expecting any more of you to arrive. I'm afraid we may not be able to find all matching parts, but we'll see what we can come up with. Let's start with the feet. See anything you like?"

It took Dean most of a day to put together a body that fit and whose colors didn't clash. As it was, his left eye was a glaring red, and the left a muddy brown, his head was a little too large for his angular body, and his wings were much too small, but he was much too happy about having a real body again to complain. St. Peter swaddled him in a robe, set a golden halo over his head and said, "Perfect. We've just got time to make the meeting. I'm sorry you won't have time to explore the place, but hey, you can't always get what you want, right?"

"I guess so," said Dean, liking the way his tongue felt during the sibilants. He had been so used to the feeling that his voice was sort of dubbed over the movement of his cartoon mouth that he had nearly forgotten what a tongue felt like. Even better, now that he thought about it, was a tongue that had never experienced cotton mouth. His whole body was clean and new, and would never experience pain or discomfort. He clicked his sandaled heels together and blushed when St. Peter looked back at him. But St. Peter was smiling, so that was all right. He skipped a couple of steps to catch up with the saint and walked with a bouncier step than he had ever seen his decapitated body use coming out of some infernal brothel.

"By the way," said St. Peter, "feel free to call me Pete. Everyone else does."

"OK, Pete," said Dean, smiling for the first time in his existence. "And you can call me Elvis."

St. Peter cast a shrewd look at Elvis and smiled. "OK, Elvis," he said. "Congratulations on being the first Elvis in heaven."

After a time they came to a huge arena with roughly the seating capacity of the Houston Astrodome. Roughly three-quarters of the seats were filled. "Looks like we're early, after all," said Dean-who-shall-now-be-called-Elvis.

"No no," said St. Peter, "I'd say we're just in time. See, there's Jesus walking up to the podium now. Let's sit down right here." He pointed at a couple of empty seats past half a dozen white-robed people. "Excuse us. Coming through." he said, as Elvis sidled past them, still grinning, his white teeth gleaming.

When they sat down, Elvis said, "Where's everyone else? Are they waiting for the late show?"

St. Peter looked surprised. "Everyone's here. You were expecting a bigger crowd?"

"But ... When I came to ... I mean ..."

"Actually, this is more than we ever expected. That's why we were so short on body parts. We had wanted everyone to have their choice." St. Peter narrowed his eyes and started to say something else. Elvis cringed inwardly, wondering how he was going to explain his whereabouts for the last several eons. At that moment, however, an unseen orchestra started up and a choir started singing some sort of anthem. When they were finished, Jesus lifted an arm and everyone applauded politely.

"Thank you, everyone, you're too kind. Really. Thank you. Thank you so much." When the applause died down, Jesus said, "I bet you're wondering why I've gathered you all here together this evening." Everyone laughed politely. "Well, it occured to me some time ago that some of us might get a little bored after awhile, what with everything being made out of gold and all, and everyone having to sing all the time, so I decided to do something a little different. I've decided we could all use a vacation.

"People of heaven," here he paused a moment, just to let the tension build. "We're going to Disneyland."

His announcement was greeted by stunned silence followed by muted whispering and finally, polite applause. Jesus held up his arm again and waited for silence. "On your way out, please remember to pick up a Hawaiian shirt and Bermuda shorts. It's bound to be hot down there. I'd hang on to your sandals if I were you, as it's bound to be a little filthy, too. Most of all, remember that we're there to have fun, but we should try to be as polite and considerate as possible to the people who are already there. Now, if no one has any questions, we'll just get started. Maestro?"

The orchestra began to play some sort of march, and everyone started to file out as if practicing for a fire drill. It took a while for the stadium to empty, since they were also changing their clothes, but eventually they all made it outside and lined up in single file. Somehow, Elvis found himself the third person in line, after Jesus and St. Peter. "Congratulations," Jesus had said, once they'd been introduced. "You're the only Elvis in heaven."

They marched for twelve days, and Elvis was overjoyed to find that he wasn't the least bit faint. On the twelfth day, Jesus raised his hand and everyone stopped in unison, as if they had practiced the maneuver a dozen times. Elvis followed Jesus' gaze and saw Johnny hiding behind a cloud with his eyes squeezed shut.

"Johnny, come forth!" said Jesus.

Johnny grimaced and stayed put.

Elvis walked over to him and put his hand on his arm. "Come on, Johnny, it's time to go." Johnny cautiously opened his eyes and looked at the hand on his arm. He followed the arm up to Elvis's face and said, "Dean? What the hell are you doing here? They told me you were in hell."

"I left," said Elvis, "but now we're going back."

"What?"

"We're going to Disneyland, Johnny."

For a moment, Johnny looked like an old man. He looked haggardly at the line of people. He was very tired. "You mean ..."

"Yes."

A tiny spark leapt to Johnny's eye. He gathered his strength and let out a feeble rebel yell. A moment of silence passed, while Johnny recovered and tried to smile, until someone else let out an equally feeble yell. Johnny and Elvis grinned at each other, and let out the biggest rebel yell they had, and everyone in line echoed them, but it was a heavenly echo, that only got stronger instead of fading away. Heaven and hell shook with yells and laughter. Everyone was gathering around Johnny and Elvis. People started to come up from hell and join the ruckus. Johnny and Elvis put their arms around each other and grinned at the camera as the credits rolled upwards in front of them.

Virgil's End

(1990)

Of stars and a hope I sing, ablaze above Earth's Paradise.
A moment's glimpse is all I've seen of them;
they are denied to those unknown to Christ.

As men may gape at a child's demise,
cut down in some horrific way before their eyes,
so stared those purgatorial shades at me—
the first to descend that blesséd mount
since God rejected Adam and his wife.

      Down in widening gyres I trod,
legs trembling with each downward step.
Only Cato, stern keeper of the mountain's foot,
begged some scrap of news from Paradise.
I answered as I could, though briefly,
of the vision in which Beatrice, my replacement, had arrived,
and of my subsequent dismissal.

The old sage bowed his head and shook his hair with sorrow.
Yet his face, when he looked up, was smiling, and he bade me send a
  message—
Not to Marcia, who had been his wife, but to Charon,
the ferryman, ward of hell's initial river.

      Oft of old had he spoken with the boatman,
Who was so near that other shore where living souls might still consider
  hope.
"Tell old crafty Charon that I think of him betimes.
The angel of the Lord, who ferries those un-damned toward their
  salvation,

keeps his eyes so firmly fixed above that he hardly stops to pass a friendly
    word."
We then embraced like brothers, parted perhaps by war, or some
    calamity.
Almost I fancied a spectral tear hovered on the threshold
of the elder statesman's eye.

Perhaps I was mistaken.

I will not here recount the horrors I endured
'tween Cato's watch and Satan's gelid lake,
nor with what wretched toil I made my weary way
up to the circle of the Frauds.
Few addressed me; none with words that bear repeating.
With only one did I desire speech:

"Ulysses, great contender, locked in fiery twain
with Diomedes, your twin in fraud: hear now my new lament.
You whose ship approached that mountain's shore,
that island where the blessed may cleanse their sins,
you have felt the inexorable force
that suffers not the near approach of pagans.

What sadness can compare to that of guide
whose equal struggle
                equal reward can never know?
Imagine the mother bear leading her young cubs
to saplings far too slender to support her ponderous weight.
Imagine her desire
            to savor also the tender leaves that sprout
Amidst the topmost branches, denied her
though her children eat their fill. So too
I led proud Dante, my child in the epic art,

to the very edge of earthly Paradise.
How I yearned to set one tired foot in those Elysian Fields,
but alas, my sins are irredeemable.
I was forced to bid farewell to prodigious Dante,
that man I would not let address you here,
     and turn my face from glory.

Odysseus, bane of Ilium, imagine my joy
at seeing once more the sun, the arcéd sky,
and the revolutions of the stars!
Gentle breezes replaced these children of Scirocco,
and for every tear there was the promise of a smile.
Forgive me if my words intensify your pain,
but only think how hard it was for me,
who was allowed to witness this first hand.
Thus was my bittersweet vision of that half—
     nay, twice-blessed country
which is the inverse of our own.

I did not think so kindly of you when I wrote.
    I apologize.
I see now that your punishment is far more worthy of compassion
then your sins were worth contempt.
Yet what strange force would pull such blasphemes from my lips,
which have but lately spoke before just heaven?
The fires of hell should not consume
acceptance of divine decree, published from the only true source: Love.
Better far to say, 'I ought not to have judged you,
who was myself so worthy to be judged.'
But I see that I detain you overlong.
Begone; resume your endless circlings:

On earth it was your only true desire."

I watched the pair depart.
How like the abandoned father did I feel!
One who has taught his offspring all he knows,
only to have him turn away, eagerly thirsting for further knowledge
when the first well he had drawn from has run dry.
I speak, of course, of Dante, whom I will hasten not to judge,
knowing that One who sits enthroned above
doth judge him much less harshly.
Indeed, his rejection of me is meet:
They who would look back when once salvation is attained
would lose themselves anew.
Lot's wife did find it thus, fleeing ruined Sodom;
a pillar of salt, she sheds no tears.
So too did lyrical Orpheus, lacking faith,
beseek Eurydice's face too soon:
Eternal separation is their doom:
Not even hell can reunite them.
I renounce therefore my heart's desire
that Dante might have clasped just once my hand
before rejecting my companionship
and enforcing my regress.

Such thoughts I forsook as I neared the eighth circle
and faced again the rocky cliffs that barred my way.
My soul filled up with fear:
In Dante's presence
I had borne courage in my shoulders,
knowing that divine decree secured our passage.
Now, as I neared the abominable Geryon,

my fear intensified, like a fire that first smolders in some leaves
then bursts into flames, growing larger and warmer,
threatening to rage uncontrolled.
              I had no guarantee that my return
to the dull company of my peers would be unhindered.
Should this gruesome beast refuse my next request,
I would spend forever with the Frauds.
The thought was too noisome to endure,
and yet the stench of Geryon himself was inescapable.
I approached him, striving to retrieve that mask of bravery
that had served me well before.
            "Back so soon?" he chortled,
"I assumed you'd prefer a somewhat longer stay
in the warmer climes above below.
Did they kick you out?
You didn't eat their apples, did you?
Amazing group of people, Christians, preaching love for all,
yet proving in the end more prejudiced than any.
Did they call you 'Caesar slayer' or 'Jovian trash'
before they sent you trotting?"
            Impassive in mien to these remarks,
I civilly begged passage to the top of the sheer cliff.
Sullen that his jibes had had no marked effect,
he proffered nonetheless to me his back,
which surface I bestrode with no little trepidation.
I clenched my knees and squeezed my eyelids shut
and cursed the beast (beneath my breath) for the turbulence of his flight.
He set me down at the top—the nadir of the seventh circle,
and I gave no thought to thanks or payment
            as I trudged unsteadily away.
His heinous laughter haunts me still.

At length the Phlegethon was crossed, the Wall of Dis re-breached,
the Styx and, and, finally, the four circles of incontinence were left
    behind.
I approached the gloomy city of my peers
disappointed (though not surprised)
that no one rushed to greet me.
I found my feet had no desire for rest but urged me on,
and through the empty dusk of limbo
to the melancholy shores of Acheron.

Charon's ferry was hardly visible through the dank and evil mist,
approaching with his boatload of the damned,
                  and while it pleased my sense of wholeness
to come as close as was allowed to the beginning of my awkward journey,
I did not relish converse with the wight.
Yet, for the sake of Cato's message, I held firm.

Discharging the chaff that peopled his craft,
the withered creature with empty eyes leaned upon his oar
and spoke:
                  "Virgil," he said, and his voice seemed sad,
"Almost I dared believe you, too, would be received by heaven,
as that Man had honored Cato, when He harrowed this foul realm.
Indeed, there is no reason I can see that you should be confined
to this abyss,
                  save only for the accident of timing,
having died a few short years before that Holy Bastard's death,
which was believed to conquer Death.
It puzzles me that when He besieged this faulty land,
he deigned ignore so many.
Surely you have committed no crime worth all this gray eternity;

were it in my power, I would ferry your shade
to a pleasanter shore than that which limits my demesne."

Then indeed I felt that I might weep,
that such compassion could be found in hell.
But no words reached my lips
to express gratitude for his charity,
so I settled for repeating Cato's message,
at which old Charon laughed, wheezing and hacking,
till I thought he must collapse.

Such sound reminded me that hell was now my home.
With a solemn, formal bow in deference to the demon's kindness,
I returned to the realm of my desperate peers.
                    Had I indeed dared hope for something more
than to act as guide through Purgatorio?
If so, that hope was triply killed with every footfall of retreat
                    from Adam's former garden.
And yet, what was my sin that I should be turned back
upon the very threshold of salvation?
Can accident of birth be grounds for such refusal?
With Dante yet beside me, my understandings had been sure,
like a goat upon the stony croppings of a ledge,
but now—how doubt confounds me!
Our candle lives are much too brief a test
on which to base eternity.

Alas, self-pity serves no end, except to heighten one's despair.
Fate's web will never come unraveled;
                    I know this to be true, and yet,
I now long only for the sight of those four stars,
those diadems in deepest velvet, that sparkle o'er Purgation's mount.

For such a sight to be made for me eternal,

I would gladly give my soul,

but that it was too soon given

to a Satan I had never heard of in my life.

[The earliest manuscripts end here, but other ancient authorities include the following postscript.]

There is little conversation among the denizens of Limbo,

but lately a blind poet has broken silences with me.

"Did you happen to see my hero on your ancient journey south?" he
     asked.

I answered as I could, though shortly,

disliking to be reminded of my past,

but he persisted in his queries until I formed this gloomy song—

The first new thing this land has ever heard.

I suppose I should be proud,

     but the soul that launched fair Helen's face was not content.

He asked, (oh, abominable question!)

whether anyone had actually asked me to leave.

To my dumbfounded stare—invisible to his blind eyes!—

he responded with another question:

"Was it possible pride alone prevented your stay?

Pride that would rather leave unnoticed than risk being asked to depart?

Were you expecting trumpets, honest Virgil? Horns to announce your
     arrival?

Did you slip away quietly, while Dante was turned, relishing the pain of
     imagined betrayal?"

I asked him to stop as civilly as I could, but in truth I wanted to strike
     him.

"What do you know of my pain?" I wanted to ask him,

but feared his answer would be, "Too much."

No matter, he was moving on to other topics,

like whether Cato really called foul Charon "crafty,"
or had I introduced the word to fit the meter.
Again I was offended, but answered him in truth:
Stern Cato had used that very word. He smiled.
"Do you honestly believe," he asked, adroitly,
"That Cato was tender, and Charon kind?
Self-pity has shuttered your eyes."

It is for art's sake that I append this postscript,
much though it pains me to sing it.
Once upon a time, the Judge who banished me to Limbo
extended mercy and did not rescind it.
I misunderstood, in pride and fear, and demurred.
We who have no demons for torture
                      here on the outskirts of hell
supply the lack by torturing ourselves:
Could I go back, had I only the courage?
Could I go back, had I only humility?
Could I go back, were I not the damnable worm
                    I will not stop insisting I am?

The Seafarer

TRANSLATED 2002

Might I wreck the truth about myself,
my lots recount, how I from days of strife
to times of struggle oft was thrown,
grim heavings of the chest I've survived,
known in the keel woehomes aplenty,
the intolerable tossings of the waves. There oft was I cast
by nightwatch narrow at the prow of the ship
whenever it drove near cliffs. Cold enclenched
were my feet, bound by frost,
by shackles of cold, that's when woes sighed
hot about my heart; but even then the hunger slit from within
my sea-weary mood. That's what no one knows,
those on land to whom things fall most fair,
how I, care-wretched, in the ice-cold sea
did dwell awinter on the exile's track,
of loved ones deprived,
behung with icicles; hail in showers flew.
There I nothing heard but roaring sea,
ice-cold wave. For awhile, the swan's song
was all I had to cheer me, the gannet's cry
and the curlew's clamor served for laughter,
the singing of the gull for draughts of mead.
Storms battered stone-cliffs there, where the tern tried to answer them
icy-feathered; many's the time an eagle screamed back at it,
dewy-feathered; but none of my helpmates
could unshrivel the shaft of my soul.

For little they believe, who in this life find joy
abiding in burgs, baleful journeys shunning,
engorged and wineglad, how I, weary often,

Wægliðend

TENTH CENTURY, AUTHOR UNKNOWN

Mæg ic be me sylfum soðgied wrecan,
siþas secgan, hu ic geswincdagum
earfoðhwile oft þrowade,
bitre breostceare gebiden hæbbe,
5 gecunnad in ceole cearselda fela,
atol yþa gewealc, þær mec oft bigeat
nearo nihtwaco æt nacan stefnan,
þonne he be clifum cnossað. Calde geþrungen
wæron mine fet, forste gebunden,
10 caldum clommum, þær þa ceare seofedun
hat ymb heortan; hungor innan slat
merewerges mod. þæt se mon ne wat
þe him on foldan fægrost limpeð,
hu ic earmcearig iscealdne sæ
15 winter wunade wræccan lastum,
winemægum bidroren,
bihongen hrimgicelum; hægl scurum fleag.
þær ic ne gehyrde butan hlimman sæ,
iscaldne wæg. Hwilum ylfete song
20 dyde ic me to gomene, ganetes hleoþor
ond huilpan sweg fore hleahtor wera,
mæw singende fore medodrince.
Stormas þær stanclifu beotan, þær him stearn oncwæð
isigfeþera; ful oft þæt earn bigeal,
25 urigfeþra; ne ænig hleomæga
feasceaftig ferð frefran meahte.
  Forþon him gelyfeð lyt, se þe ah lifes wyn
gebiden in burgum, bealosiþa hwon,
wlonc ond wingal, hu ic werig oft

in the sea-lanes chose to dwell.
Nightshade has deepened, to the north it has snowed,
ice locks in the land, hail has fallen on earth,
of corns the coldest. Therefore now the knocking
at my heart is pleading, that I toward wretched currents,
salty tumults, should set out alone;
moans my heart's desire, every time
      forth to fair, that I far hence
a stranger's land should seek.
Because no one so spirit proud in all the earth
be their gifts however good, their youthfulness so hearty,
their deeds so doughty, no matter how loyal to their lord,
takes to their seafaring without concern
for what their Lord might will to do.
Their mind is not on the harp, nor on the winning of rings,
nor on the joy of a spouse, nor on the bliss of the world,
nor on aught else save the rolling of the waves,
but ever they have a longing who set a course on water.
Groves take on blossoms, beautify burgs,
brighten fields, hasten on the world;
all of this exhorts the mind's eager
      heart toward the journey by which it thinks
      toward floodways far to embark.
Such the cuckoo urges with sorrowful voice,
sings summer's ward, bodes sorrow,
bitter in the breast's hoard. That's what no one knows,
at ease in heart, what some others suffer,
they for whom the exile's track lies widest.
      That's why my heart now flies beyond its cage,
my soul with the sea-flood
over the whales' home tacks wide,
earth forsaking, comes oft to me
ravenous and greedy, yells the lone flyer,

30 in brimlade   bidan sceolde.
     Nap nihtscua,   norþan sniwde,
     hrim hrusan bond,   hægl feol on eorþan,
     corna caldast.   Forþon cnyssað nu
     heortan geþohtas,   þæt ic hean streamas,
35 sealtyþa gelac   sylf cunnige;
     monað modes lust   mæla gehwylce
     ferð to feran,   þæt ic feor heonan
     elþeodigra   eard gesece.
     Forþon nis þæs modwlonc   mon ofer eorþan,
40 ne his gifena þæs god,   ne in geoguþe to þæs hwæt,
     ne in his dædum to þæs deor,   ne him his dryhten to þæs hold,
     þæt he a his sæfore   sorge næbbe,
     to hwon hine dryhten   gedon wille.
     Ne biþ him to hearpan hyge   ne to hringþege,
45 ne to wife wyn   ne to worulde hyht,
     ne ymbe owiht elles,   nefne ymb yða gewealc,
     ac a hafað longunge   se þe on lagu fundað.
     Bearwas blostmum nimað,   byrig fægriað,
     wongas wlitigað,   woruld onetteð;
50 ealle þa gemoniað   modes fusne
     sefan to siþe,   þam þe swa þenceð
     on flodwegas   feor gewitan.
     Swylce geac monað   geomran reorde,
     singeð sumeres weard,   sorge beodeð
55 bitter in breosthord.   þæt se beorn ne wat,
     esteadig secg,   hwæt þa sume dreogað
     þe þa wræclastas   widost lecgað.
          Forþon nu min hyge hweorfeð   ofer hreþerlocan,
     min modsefa   mid mereflode
60 ofer hwæles eþel   hweorfeð wide,
     eorþan sceatas,   cymeð eft to me
     gifre ond grædig,   gielleð anfloga,

whets on the whaleway my heart irresistably
over the waters of the sea. Because hotter to me
are the joys of the Lord than this dead life,
not long on land. I believe not at all
that before him earthen wealth ever stands.
Always the threesome inevitable,
before the moment of horror, at the crossroads becomes
addle or age or swordedge
to the fey departing, wrests life away.
Therefore, that is for all folk noble the eulogy,
the praise of the living, the obituary that is best,
that they worked, ere they were on their way,
strove valiantly on earth with fiends malicious,
dour deeds to the devil opposed,
that those of elders born later should sing
and his praise thence should live with the angels
to the end of time, eternal life's glory,
joy with the hosts.
                        The days are departed
all vainglorious, of earthly riches;
no longer be there kings, or kaisers
or goldgiving, such as once there were,
when among themselves the highest glories they achieved,
and on lordliest power they lived.
Perished is all that host, their dreams have departed,
weaker ones remain and the world bears them,
they live in it by toil. Glory is humbled,
earthen nobility ages and fades,
as does everyone beyond middle earth.
Old age overtakes them, blanches their face,
the age-grayed mourns, remembering friends,
the children of princes, given the world.
No profit then the flesh home, when life is lost,

hweteð on hwælweg   hreþer unwearnum
ofer holma gelagu.   Forþon me hatran sind
65 dryhtnes dreamas   þonne þis deade lif,
læne on londe.   Ic gelyfe no
þæt him eorðwelan   ece stondað.
Simle þreora sum   þinga gehwylce,
ær his tid aga,   to tweon weorþeð;
70 adl oþþe yldo   oþþe ecghete
fægum fromweardum   feorh oðþringeð.
Forþon þæt bið eorla gehwam   æftercweþendra
lof lifgendra   lastworda betst,
þæt he gewyrce,   ær he on weg scyle,
75 fremum on foldan   wið feonda niþ,
deorum dædum   deofle togeanes,
þæt hine ælda bearn   æfter hergen,
ond his lof siþþan   lifge mid englum
awa to ealdre,   ecan lifes blæd,
80 dream mid dugeþum.

        Dagas sind gewitene,
ealle onmedlan   eorþan rices;
næron nu cyningas   ne caseras
ne goldgiefan   swylce iu wæron,
þonne hi mæst mid him   mærþa gefremedon
85 ond on dryhtlicestum   dome lifdon.
Gedroren is þeos duguð eal,   dreamas sind gewitene,
wuniað þa wacran   ond þas woruld healdaþ,
brucað þurh bisgo.   Blæd is gehnæged,
eorþan indryhto   ealdað ond searað,
90 swa nu monna gehwylc   geond middangeard.
Yldo him on fareð,   onsyn blacað,
gomelfeax gnornað,   wat his iuwine,
æþelinga bearn,   eorþan forgiefene.
Ne mæg him þonne se flæschoma,   þonne him þæt feorg losað,

either to taste the sweet or to feel the sore,
to stir the hand or to think with the mind.
Though the grave they should wish to strew with gold
the siblings one for another, to bury among the dead,
with various treasures that they wish for each other,
no profit there for souls full of sin
gold to yoke for the terror of God,
when they hide it early while they live here.

    Great is the terror of the creator, for the earth turns before him;
he established stolid ground,
the earth's face and the high heaven.
Doltish are they who dread not the Lord; they come to their death
    unprepared.
Blessed are they who live humbly; they come to the mercy of heaven,
the creator who establishes courage in them, because they believed in his might.
They should steer their strong moods, and that on the straight path to hold,
and on pledges true, manners clean,
Everyone in equal measure should hold off,
with the dear and with the dire, ruin,
though they might wish upon the one the fulness of flames
or on the pyre burned
their well-earned friend; fate be stronger,
the creator mightier than anyone's intention.
Let us plan where we should have our home
and then think how thither we should come,
and then each of us should strive that we too be allowed
into the eternal blessedness;
where life is depending on the love of the Lord,
high in heaven. After that we should thank the holy one
that he honors us, wondrous elder
eternal Lord, in all time.
        Amen.

95 ne swete forswelgan   ne sar gefelan,

    ne hond onhreran   ne mid hyge þencan.

    þeah þe græf wille   golde stregan

    broþor his geborenum,   byrgan be deadum,

    maþmum mislicum   þæt hine mid wille,

100 ne mæg þære sawle   þe biþ synna ful

    gold to geoce   for godes egsan,

    þonne he hit ær hydeð   þenden he her leofað.

        Micel biþ se meotudes egsa,   forþon hi seo molde oncyrreð;

    se gestaþelade   stiþe grundas,

105 eorþan sceatas   ond uprodor.

    Dol biþ se þe him his dryhten ne ondrædeþ;   cymeð him se deað unþinged.

    Eadig bið se þe eaþmod leofaþ;   cymeð him seo ar of heofonum,

    meotod him þæt mod gestaþelað,   forþon he in his meahte gelyfeð.

    Stieran mon sceal strongum mode,   ond þæt on staþelum healdan,

110 ond gewis werum,   wisum clæne,

    scyle monna gehwylc   mid gemete healdan

    wiþ leofne ond wið laþne   bealo,

    þeah þe he hine wille fyres   fulne

    oþþe on bæle   forbærnedne

115 his geworhtne wine.   Wyrd biþ swiþre,

    meotud meahtigra   þonne ænges monnes gehygd.

    Uton we hycgan   hwær we ham agen,

    ond þonne geþencan   hu we þider cumen,

    ond we þonne eac tilien,   þæt we to moten

120 in þa ecan   eadignesse,

    þær is lif gelong   in lufan dryhtnes,

    hyht in heofonum.   þæs sy þam halgan þonc,

    þæt he usic geweorþade,   wuldres ealdor,

    ece dryhten,   in ealle tid.

125   Amen.

The Trucker

(2002)

Allow me to drive this old truth ballad home,
tell you my travels, how I through dogged days
and doggeder nights have often driven,
beset by bitter heartburn, by my gullet's indignation,
grossly compounded by the arrhythmic thumpings of bumpy macadam,
    where often I've clung,
through anxious, predawn hours, to the truck's big wheel
when the road wound taut around the mountains.

Though hemorrhoid-riddled
was my big rear end, burned by itching,
by rashes inflamed—the emergency flares
of my sphincter—inexplicable yearnings would rise in my soul
from the depths of my road-weary mood.

That's what nobody knows,
for whom days at the office tick past like pleasant dreams,
how I, arms aching, in between snowdrifts,
spent winters on the soul-taxing road,
forsaking companions, abuzz from caffeine,
while hailstones clattered on the hood.

There I heard naught but the whirring of wheels,
the whine of the engine, CB static. At times Ronnie Milsap
was a night on the town, Merle Haggard
or Kathy Mattea raucous laughter in a bar,
and Patsy Cline was my cold, draft beer.
When windstorms beat their fists against the trailer there,

Johnny Cash might try to quell them with his fourth-gear growl,
or Willie Nelson with his third-gear vibrato,
yet none of my FM good buddies
could unclench my white-knuckled grip.

How little some people comprehend,
content in their suburbs, avoiding the cross-country run,
one-upping each other with sports cars and giddy from Merlot,
why I, most often exhausted,
chose instead to dwell in the truck lanes.

The semis have turned on their high beams; it's snowing in Sioux Falls.
Rime obscures road signs; for Fargo the forecast is hail—
brittlest of ball bearings. So now the air horn of my spirit
blares its piercing call, that I, toward unplowed roads,
black ice and fish-tailing cars, should travel on alone.
Thus my heart implores me, all the time,
outbound to drive, toward that faraway, uncanny city—
not found on any map—where lies the home I seek.

For no one so reckless in all the world,
no matter how spotless their record, or how many miles they've logged,
how green and overconfident, or skillful at outsmarting smokies,
embarks on long journeys without pondering anew
what the Lord has in store for them this time.
They don't care what they're missing on network TV; they aren't hoping
     to win sweepstakes
or someone's affection. Nor do they pine for the comforts of routine.
All they're concerned with is wheels on the tarmac;
their ultimate destination their only desire.

When blossoms infuse winter's branches, beautifying cities

and brightening fields, the world skips merrily along.
But such things only quicken the mind's eager yearning
for the streets that lead to the toll booths,
beyond which must surely lie freedom.
That's what the mourning dove's song is about, its aching lament;
it calls to forestall summer's sorrow,
the pang in the heart's empty tank.

That's what no one understands
whose hearts are free from care: why others among us long endure
the lonesome, endless highway's single lane.
That's why my soul slips often from its cage,
why my hope irresistibly steers me
away to where triple trailers roam, bypassing populous cities.
It returns to me, greedy and eager, and howls like an ambulance siren,
whetting my heart's irrepressible urge to drive where the wide loads
     rumble,
out on the sweeping freeways of the plains.

Because, for me, the heavy-duty battery of the Lord
has starting power stronger than this dead life.
Those smoke-detector nine-volts aren't any use
when your house is already afire.
Don't you know how soon you'll be ambushed
by any one of the goblins three?
Ailing, aging or the aim of a gun
will twist off your life like a bottle cap.
And what will folk say *in memoriam?*

There's only one way to a lengthier eulogy, while your steering wheel's
     still in your grasp:
take a detour to some virtuous deed before it's too late,

a kindness or two, despite all your demons,
something decent to dash in the devil's own face,
so that downtrodden folk might have reason to thank you,
and your praise after that should survive with the angels
for all of eternity—never-ending glory
in the company of heaven.

Gone are the days,
all golden and gleaming, of the boomtown;
gone are the barons, the magnates, the entrepreneurs,
the erecting of hospitals, libraries and museums—
philanthropy as a means of one-upmanship—
and feasting each other like kings.
All of them are food for worms, now; their schemes have passed away.
Lesser folk remain, whom the world has not yet disgorged;
their days are replete with nibbling.

The illustrious are mortified, the powerful grow old;
even their memory fades from our mind.
So perish we all who pace out our claim on this perilous rock;
old age bends our spine and blanches our face.

The gray-haired grieve, remembering friends—
the children of privilege, given the world.
There's no power left, once these flesh suits are empty,
to taste what's sweet or to feel what's sore,
to grasp with the hand or to think with the brain.
Though their coffins be made out of bullet-proof glass, and their bodies
frozen by doctors, to be revived in some fictional future
with diversified portfolios set up for them—they wish this on each other!
No profit there for sinners—
the vengeance of God versus science and wealth—

while they live, people hope such things hide them.

From the fear of the Lord the whole world turns away,
though each grain of sand be God's careful creation
and each tiny wisp of a cloud.

Dolts are the ones who don't fear God; they die with their arms at their
     sides.
Yet happy are they who are humble and lowly, who lift their limbs to the
     Lord's lovingkindness.
The creator will hold out a steadying hand to any who reach out to grab it.

We all need to pilot our passions, to keep them between the white lines,
with promises kept and consciences pure,
looking out for each other, to fend off the downfall
of friend and foe alike.
Though we might wish the fire of hell upon foes,
and a memorial flame for the friends that stood by us—
fate is stronger, the creator mightier
than anyone's intention.

So let's turn our grilles toward the home that we long for
and map out the quickest route there,
that we may arrive—with our cargo intact—where those who are
     blessed take it easy.
There we'll live long in the care of the Lord,
who cruises the highest of byways.

We give thanks for the license to follow you home,
Gracious God and glorious dispatcher.

Road without end.
Amen.

Hildiah & the Donkey

(1995), INSPIRED BY 1 KINGS 13

"Hildiah," said the Lord, "There comes a man I want you to slay." God was a snow-white lamb, such as Hildiah loved to eat. He wondered, half-seriously, if the Lord would mind being eaten. Hildiah had been lying in the shade of a vine when the lamb curled up fearlessly between his great tawny forepaws.

"My Lord?" said Hildiah, recognizing the lightning-brightness of the wool.

"There comes a man," repeated the lamb, burying his face in Hildiah's mane, "who is great in my kingdom. Him I wish you to slay this very evening."

Hildiah's chest surged with wounded pride. "Just one, my Lord? With a single swipe of my paw I could cave in the skull of a bull; one man will provide no challenge at all." Hildiah yearned to be like Phrygeon, who had killed five hundred hyenas though but the runt of the litter. Hildiah was no runt, but he would fain his deeds be similarly remembered. With great effort, he put away his disappointment. "Thy will be done, my Lord," he said.

"This man," said the Almighty, scratching the top of his head against Hildiah's chin, "has been sent by me to prophecy death to the priests of the altars, whom Jeroboam has appointed from among the people, for verily their bones shall be burnt on the very altars at which they sacrifice. For I am the Lord. They shall have no other gods before me."

"Amen," said Hildiah, "Lord, have mercy."

"I have further instructed him not to eat or drink anything in this place, nor to return by the way he came, for I am the Lord."

"Amen," said Hildiah, "Lord, have mercy."

"Nevertheless, he has been deceived by another who bears my name, and is even now at sup with him. For this reason, he will never be buried with his ancestors but will die in Israel, though he belongs to Judah."

"Amen," said Hildiah, "er—"

The LORD stood up and stretched his tender frame. "Here he comes now."

"Lord," said Hildiah, "What is his name?"

"That," said the LORD God Most High, "is a secret, and will remain so until the end."

The lamb kissed Hildiah on the muzzle, then tottered away.

Hildiah stood also and shook his mane. At that moment, from over a ridge, appeared the man of whom the LORD had spoken. He was riding a donkey who, at the sight of Hildiah, hesitated, and seemed to sag. A terrible suffering was in its eyes, and Hildiah was moved. What had the LORD told the donkey? Did it know that its master would be slain today, from off its very back? The man himself seemed lost in thought, uncaring whether he was moving or not, nor in which direction.

Hildiah had always admired donkeys, ever since hearing the story of Balaam's ass, the one who had refused to carry his master forward when it saw the angel of death. Three times it turned aside, courageously enduring its master's whip. Would this donkey turn aside also? Hildiah crouched beside a vine and waited.

With a sigh that was loud enough for Hildiah to hear, the donkey resumed its walking. Hildiah's stomach growled, followed by his throat, as his hunting instinct erased all doubts and uncertainties. A feast lay before him, ordained by the Lord himself. Hildiah would do as the LORD had bade.

He charged. Still, the man seemed oblivious. He gathered himself for a leap, and the man at last looked up. In the instant before Hildiah's bottom teeth caught beneath the man's chin, Hildiah beheld the elongated pupils of the lamb.

With an awkward somersault, he rolled off the body and disengaged his teeth from the skull. He stood and considered the ravaged visage of his prey. It was crumpled, but still recognizable. Hildiah's tongue still held the impression of the man's nose. The donkey took no notice of him, but was tenderly wiping blood from the ruined face with its own cheeks. Hildiah lowered his haunches and watched the donkey's ministrations with furrowed brow. Side by side, the two kept vigil until nightfall, when another man, and another donkey, came to bear the man of God away.

While the other man dismounted some distance off for fear of Hildiah, the other donkey continued toward the body, and for a moment the three of them nuzzled each other in mute and mutual sorrow, until Hildiah's emotions overwhelmed him, and he loped away.

For the rest of his life, the sight of a donkey would overwhelm him with grief, and he never again sought renown.

That Critical Absence

(2013)

Alef scanned the pitiless sky for any hint of cloud, strained her ears for the slightest drip of water, but heard only—she spun, stabbing something hairy and heaving it over her head. With desperate haste, she pounced upon the creature's groin to catch the last few drops of piss. There wasn't much, but the moisture would keep her sharp for a few more hours. She stood, assessing its pelt and meat, and wished only that it had put up a better fight.

It was big enough to have crushed her, yet its attack had been clumsy as a cub's, and what kind of creature has cubs that size? She glanced around almost nervou—the swipe of her knife barely halted the monster's charge. As the behemoth circled, one eyeball inches from the tip of her blade, Alef noted rows of swollen teats. Risking a glance at the corpse, its youth now unmistakable, she recognized the imminence of her own demise.

Her blade would not avail her, so she dropped it. The creature's eyes narrowed.

Its hesitation made Alef wonder if it, too, longed for a worthier opponent. She considered the depth of a mother's grief and rage and let her shoulders sag.

"Very well," she said. "May our battle bring you peace."

With a somersault, she retrieved her blade, lunged recklessly, retreated, feinted to one side, dodged the predictab—her braid yanked her backwards, so she sliced it off and tumbled into the brittle bracken.

While the monster spat and clawed at the leather-bound plait in its teeth, Alef sprinted forward. Stepping on its brow, she sprang upon its shoulders, stabbing repeatedly at its impervious pelt. It gyred onto its back, but she log-rolled it and leapt clear, dove as it lunged, and plunged her blade up under its chin.

It was all she could give: a scar to commemorate a mother's vengeance. With a flick of its neck and a snap of its jaws, Alef's knife was wrenched from her grasp and her head was separated from her hips. Her spirit lingered just long enough to hear a triumphant bellow dissolve into a heartbreaking howl.

The taste of blood and bile turned bitter in Tav's throat. Her feckless child was avenged, but still as dead, and who would father more? She had slain her mate for threatening the last of their litter, but now her runt was gone where no threats dared. She turned to the assassin and sniffed the space between its shoulders and pelvis—that critical absence—and wondered what had inspired its doomed attack against impossible odds.

Her wounded chin stung like fire, like ice, but the deeper pain was deep in her stomach, where festered the knowledge that she was the cause of her species' extinction. What else could she do but ferret out the aching remorse with her teeth? Her purpose was fulfilled, she stretched upon the arid ground and offered her intestines to the sky.

The sky, appeased, sent rain.

Ersatz Story

(1988)

Michael Ersatz didn't get invited to many parties. He spent most of his time writing short, controversial treatises on, for instance, the many uses of sawdust. I say controversial, but it's not as if anyone had ever read them. He refused to publish his work until he had written something as close to perfect as man's nature would allow.

To return to the subject of parties, not many were held in that particular corner of Alaska at the time Michael Ersatz lived there. In fact, unless some primeval Inuits had ever celebrated the death of a polar bear in the vicinity, there had never been a party there in the history of mankind.

Before that, I cannot speculate.

Michael came to this spot early in 1983, when he was barely twenty-seven. A thriving community had failed to spring up around him, and that was just the way he wanted it. He was rarely unhappy and never hungry, and he had Sheeba to keep him company, so he couldn't complain: He was a dedicated writer.

Rachel Harrier lived in New Jersey. Her father, Richard, lived in Los Angeles and her mother, Felicia, in Colorado. She was 23, fresh out of college, and she hadn't the least idea how she was going to keep herself occupied for the rest of her life. At the moment she was a cashier at a local supermarket wondering why the hell she had chosen English as her major. Even Marylou Fresnehan had a terrific job as a research assistant for a firm that designed houses. She had been a History major. Most of her other friends, of course, were already making $35,000 dollars a year in management positions for giant corporations. Rachel thought about that every time she punched in at the Stop 'n' Shop in downtown Sculhaven.

Her father had several times—no, let's make that dozens of times—offered her a position in his highly lucrative company in Los Angeles which manufactured small, cloth covered squares of rubber used for "mice," the little cursor controllers used with many of the latest computers. For each dozen of his offers, she had said "no" an average of 28 times. She didn't want any more handouts from her father. Nevertheless, she was getting tired of eating Kraft Macaroni and Cheese every night so that she could save money for a real house and a new car. Preferably within twenty miles of London. She had many dreams.

None of them had anything to do with any part of Alaska.

Philip Lazarus, ex-coal miner and father of four, was comatose at age 43. He had had one of those near-death experiences (some time after that final, mind-wrenching realization that he was not about to be rescued, that he was going to die in the stifling pit that had been his workplace for the past 25 years), and it had been a decidedly strange experience.

It had been more detailed than most he'd heard about. There was the same brilliant whiteness, the feeling of weightlessness, the whole gamut of symptoms that characterize the after-life. There was even Jesus, resplendent in all his unbearable glory, beckoning to him, saying, "Lazarus, come forth," like the jokes his friends sometimes made, but instead of floating towards Him, he floated away, felt once more the cold weight of his body—poisoned, asphyxiated, dehydrated—dead in all respects except reality. He nevertheless opened his eyes, stood up and walked through the gaping, dust-choked hole that hadn't been there when he died. Amid his cheering coworkers was his tear-stained wife. He stumbled into her arms, rolled his eyes, and sank once more into darkness.

He had been a miner all his life. All of his higher goals had centered around providing for his family. His one dream was to die at home, asleep, dear Helen at his side.

But that would come later.

"I tell ya, that Ersatz fellow is a Russian spy. Three years, he's been out there, and the only words he's ever spoken to me are 'Hi' and 'Thank you.' Completely ignores anything I say to him. 'Tain't natural."

Thus spake Jeb Tarkin, sole proprietor of "Jeb's, The Biggest Supermarket For A Hundred Miles." (Need it even be mentioned that it was the only supermarket for a hundred miles? I think not.) Jeb's audience that night was a small but devoted group of men who sat around the big Mother Bear stove as though they were in a Mercantile from the old West, or a quaint little general store from backwoods New England. But it was indeed a supermarket. There were big fluorescent lights, and rows (though sparsely stocked) of all kinds of foodstuffs, and even an electronic cash register.

Jeb had inherited a fair amount of money when a rich uncle from New York had died in a night club fire. Not knowing what else to do with it, he had forsaken his prospecting days and built Jeb's. The 2,000 scattered residents of Dorf, Alaska, often found it obnoxiously like the supermarkets they thought they had left behind, but the place nevertheless did respectably well. The seven men, whose average age was 82, nodded their heads in solemn agreement.

Michael Ersatz made the two day trip to Jeb's every two months.

Philip Lazarus came out of his coma understandably feeling reborn. It was late at night, and the old man one bed over was rasping softly. Philip lay awake under the unfocused clarity of the moonlight sifting through the window, quietly reveling in the miracle that had brought him to this moment.

A slight, almost imperceptible gasp alerted him to the presence of someone else in the room. He turned his head, amazed at how easily such movement came, and beheld the shining eyes of Helen.

She was sitting in a chair, next to the door. He had no doubt that she had been sitting there for as long as he had been unconscious, though he wouldn't find out until some time later that it had been two weeks. How she had managed to convince the staff to let her sit there long past visiting hours he had no way of knowing, but he praised his new-found God she had.

"Helen," he tried to say, though what came out was a formless croak.

"I'm here," she said, leaning toward him and finding his hand. When he woke the next morning (not remembering the moment sleep had retaken him), Helen would still be there, quietly holding his hand, the salt tracks of dried tears marring her cheeks.

Philip Lazarus had never been happier in his life.

Richard Harrier was disappointed. He had always cherished the notion of one day having a son to carry on the family business, but fate had seen fit to grace him with a daughter. That first disappointment had been ameliorated by the realization that, "Hell, it's the eighties, women can do such things nowadays. They can even carry on the family name if they want to."

But Rachel didn't want to join the firm. She was off in New Jersey, of all places, ringing up groceries. He had countless times implored her to take hold of the golden opportunity he was holding out to her, but she continually rebuffed him, preferring to sink on her own than swim with the help of "Daddy."

Independence was one thing; stupidity was quite another.

He would give her one more month to rethink her position, and then he would take matters into his own hands. He was damned if he was going to watch his only daughter drown while he stood on the dock, ineffectually throwing life preservers at her. He was going to by-god jump in and pull her out, whether she wanted to or not.

He was that kind of guy.

Michael Ersatz was finally ready. After three years of solitary writing, he finally had something finished and worthwhile. It was a short piece, a mere two pages long, but he had been honing it almost constantly throughout the past nine months. To Michael's eyes, the piece was so polished he could see the reflection of his face in it. It was the culmination of a lifetime's struggle to write something staggeringly worthwhile.

He would send his only copy to Mother Earth News with a short cover letter, and patiently await the letter that would make or break his life. He would not countenance rejection, even once. Better to die than to live in a world too blind to recognize perfection.

Tomorrow morning, he would ready himself for the two day journey, and drive his snow cat to Dorf. There he would deliver the manuscript into the hands of the Postmaster personally. And perhaps, after the long hard months that would trudge past in the interim, he would once again be able to walk among his fellow man and discover what had happened in the last three years.

Michael Ersatz spent the rest of the night preparing for his journey, carefully packing his best clothes, his tent, his sleeping bag and firewood, along with all the food and other little things he and Sheeba might conceivably need. Then he got into bed and pretended that he was sleeping rather than fidgeting for the rest of the night.

Felicia Harrier read over the divorce papers with grim satisfaction. She was finally on her way back to being Felicia Carpenter, and she loved it. She was finally getting rid of the arrogant son of a bitch she had been forced to call a husband for the past 24 years. She was finally going to be free.

But she was worried about Rachel. If only she'd get out of that horrid "Garden State" and come live with her in Aspen. They could have so much fun together, skiing, picking up guys, throwing wild parties . . .

She would come; Felicia was sure of it, if only the girl's bastard of a father wouldn't keep pressuring her to move to Los Angeles to carry on the stupid "family business." Of all the absurd products in the world, she thought "mouse pads" had to be the silliest. She always pictured little white mice scurrying around in their own apartments inviting friends over to share a joint and listen to the Grateful Dead. Her almost ex-husband was insane, and she was damned if he was going to force Rachel to do anything she didn't want to.

She decided then and there to take whatever steps necessary to ensure that Dick would never succeed in forcing their daughter into accepting his job offer. She didn't know how, but she'd do it, and then Rachel would be free, too, and they could both live happily ever after.

Felicia smiled to herself and set her mind to scheming.

Much to his dismay, Philip found that he was now a celebrity. Gone were his dreams of settling down with his family, receiving Workman's Comp and living out the rest of his days in peace. He was suddenly forced to do on-the-spot interviews for radio, TV, and newspapers. He was deluged with letters and visitors of all kinds, both praising and condemning him, though he knew not why. He was the subject of national controversy, and there seemed no way to put a stop to it.

So he raised his head as best he could and tried to ride out the storm.

One man had come to his house with a shotgun, screaming incoherently about a daughter and the religious freaks she called her friends and how much he hated all the stupid sheep in the world who would believe anything the television told them, and how all the people who were instigating these things for the sake of greed and avarice ought to be shot. Luckily, there had been a policeman handy who had managed to subdue the poor man before he caused any damage. Philip Lazarus was completely bewildered by the whole spectacle. He began to wish that he had never mentioned the part about his near-death experience. He wished he had had the foresight to keep the story among his own family.

Unfortunately, the storm was about to become a hurricane.

The storm that bore down on Michael Ersatz and his St. Bernard, Sheeba, was of a different sort altogether. His was a blistering, biting blizzard of the first magnitude. Sheeba was huddled in the luggage compartment of the huge snow machine, whimpering softly. He was going to have to stop soon if he wanted to live through the night.

"Dammitall," he muttered, "why didn't I bother to check the weather before I left? A simple glance to the sky would have shown me that I had a world class blizzard coming. Probably last three days, too. Ah, well, we're just going to have to tough it out for a few days; we'll manage."

"How ya doin' back there, Sheeba?" came the distant-sounding cry from beyond the cramped luggage compartment. For a moment it confused Sheeba; she had almost never heard her master speak. It worried her that he should talk now, especially with that touch of joy edging his voice. He was a doleful man, prone to long spells of sitting in chairs doing absolutely nothing. Sheeba wondered vaguely if he was mad. She uttered a short, incomprehensible bark, which ended in a little whine, and curled up a little tighter. She hoped they would stop soon. She could feel the distant nerve endings of her tail starting to freeze and knew it wouldn't be long before the rest of her followed.

She wished she had more faith in her normally taciturn master.

Rachel Harrier yelled in frustration. Her stupid parents were going to be the death of her. Her father had sent her a one-way plane ticket to Los Angeles, her mother a one-way ticket to Denver. Both assured her that she'd be happier this way.

Well, she was old enough to make her own decisions, thank you very much. If New Jersey had turned into a dead end (which it certainly had), she'd find her own way out of it. She ripped both the tickets in half and flushed them down the toilet (just so she couldn't tape the pieces together later). Then she grabbed her checkbook and walked to the bank. Her life savings came to $8,865.32. It would not last long.

She rented a Ford Tempo from Avis,* as it was the smallest car she could find that would hold all her stuff, and drove it home feeling the way she imagined successful people must feel. She felt that she might actually make it in this hard, cold world, once she found someplace that would be right for her.

Why she chose Alaska she didn't know; it just seemed right. It was the "last American frontier." The one place left that was still the land of opportunity, the final bastion of the American ideal.

And it sounded like a neat place to live.

Philip Lazarus was homesick. There he was, eating dinner at his own table, in his own house, with his own family, and he felt seriously homesick. Maybe it was because of the three reporters that had interviewed him today, three being a major drop from the last three weeks. The whole thing seemed to be blowing away, but it still seemed far from over. The quiet, earthy aura that had made this house a home was gone, probably forever, all because of the simple incident that had saved his life.

Not that he was ungrateful; he supposed it was a small price to pay, but it still seemed somehow unfair. People miraculously recovered in hospitals everyday. They died, went to heaven and came back all the time. What was so special about him?

He looked at Helen, and at each of his four children, ranging in age from 13 to 18. He thought about how all this must be affecting them.

"How would you all like to go to Alaska?" he said, as surprised by the suggestion as the rest of his family.

"Do ya mean it, Dad?" said the youngest boy, making Philip realized that he hadn't seen him smile for almost two weeks.

"Of course I do. If no one here would mind."

No one did.

After three days, the storm decided to get worse.

Michael and Sheeba were wrapped around each other with the sleeping bag over both of them. The tent had been a bitch to set up, but it managed to keep out the wind and most of the snow. It didn't do diddly against the cold. The small, battery-operated quartz heater kept the tent lighted, if not warm, and there was food enough to last three more days.

Michael was beginning to worry they might starve.

Sheeba was not unhappy. It had been rough going for awhile, but her master had finally come to his senses. She was warm and fed, and she kind of liked it here. If only the wind didn't howl quite so much, the place would be perfect. She yawned happily and tried to get back to sleep.

"Not a great omen for the completion of my article," her master mused, "but better than none at all. At least the universe seems to have noticed."

Sheeba did her best to thump her tail once or twice in spite of the cramped quarters. She had grown used to his unusual loquaciousness, and it no longer worried her. The smell of change was in the air, and she had decided that perhaps change was just what they needed. It was curious that the smell hadn't gone away when they got here: she had assumed they were here to stay. But her faith was restored a measure, and she was content to let things come as they would. For now, anyway.

Why am I here? thought Rachel, as her somewhat-the-worse-for-wear Tempo pulled into the only hotel in Dorf, Alaska. The Tempo was covered with ice, and ice was about the only thing she had seen for the last twenty-five miles. She quickly decided that the "final bastion of the American ideal" could get bent: She was leaving for Orlando the next morning.

Of course, she was down to $5,132.82 now, and she didn't have any way of getting more, so she decided maybe she'd brave it out for awhile until she could replenish her funds a little. A month, maybe—no more.

She took a deep breath and held it as she ran out the door, tried to get her suitcase out of the trunk as quickly as possible, and ran into the hotel. She was surprised at how little the cold seemed to abate inside.

"No room," said the old man behind the counter, merrily.

"But—" she said.

"Not to worry, though, there are plenty of suites."

She looked at him as though he must be mad, and he chuckled. "Isn't every day I can try that joke out on someone new," he said, tipping her a wink. How long will you be staying in Dorf, Missy?"

"Not too long," she said hopefully," I should be out of here tomorrow."

"That's too bad," said the man, "that's just too bad."

"Yeah, well . . ." she said, feeling more and more awkward by the moment. "Can I have a suite then?"

"Sure," said the man, holding out a bowl of mints. "Help yourself."

"I mean—"

"I know what you mean, Missy, I'm just having some fun. How does thirty-eight dollars a night sound?"

"Fine, " said Rachel, as icily as her car. She took the key the grinning old man handed her and stomped up the stairs, her suitcase bumping behind her. This place has got to go, she thought. There's no way I'm staying here more than a week.

It would be awhile before she realized she was lying.

Philip Lazarus walked into the same hotel fifteen minutes later, and was treated to the same spiel.

"How much is a suite?" he asked, in response to the first little joke.

"They're free," said the man, holding out the bowl.

"I'll take three," said Philip, and promptly turned and motioned his family in. "And have someone bring our bags to our rooms."

Philip was in no mood for games.

"Of course, I was only kidding, sir," said the man, hastily. "Suites are forty-five dollars a night."

Philip placed two fifties on the counter and silently dared the man to ask for more. The man coughed uncomfortably and reached for three adjacent keys—to the third floor. Philip granted him his petty victory and waved his family upstairs.

"And don't forget the luggage," he called down, just before he passed out of earshot.

"And don't forget the luggage," the poor man mimicked, making a mental note to put a little extra baking soda in the muffins the next morning. He got the luggage.

Fifteen minutes after that, Michael Ersatz trudged in with Sheeba. Here, at last was a man the clerk could deal with.

"Could I have a sweet, Charlie?"

"Have seven," said the man, glad to see someone in a good mood.

"Thanks," said Philip, counting out seven mints. "I needed that."

"Room 13?" asked the man, reaching for the key.

"Make that room seven, Charlie, and keep the change." He put a fifty on the counter and wished Charlie a good night.

"Good night, Mr. Ersatz, and thank you." The fifty came within four dollars of the actual price for the Lazarus family's three suites. Michael was a good man, no matter what other people might say.

Once in his room, Michael shrugged off his backpack and sat down on the bed. The Post Office was closed, but that was all right. He had made it through four days of the worst blizzard in ten years, and although it had taken nearly an hour to dig himself and his vehicle out of the snow, the remainder of the journey had been largely uneventful. It was good to be back among people again.

Sheeba barked and wagged her tail expectantly. He reached into his pocket and dug out the ground beef he always wrapped in foil for the end of such journeys. It was still a bit frozen, but Sheeba wouldn't mind. He unwrapped it and tossed it onto the floor. Sheeba wrestled with it for five minutes, and it was gone.

"Good dog," said Michael.

Good man, thought Sheeba.

They slept for the next sixteen hours, and when they woke up, it was to the most hideous sound imaginable.

"What in God's name is that?!" cried Michael, over the sound of Sheeba's howling. It had been three years since either had heard a siren.

Jeb's supermarket was burning.

15,463,978,004,328,597,878,431,256,789 (Fifteen octillion, four hundred and sixty-three septillion, nine hundred and seventy-eight sextillion, four quintillion, three hundred and twenty-eight quadrillion, five hundred and ninety-seven trillion, eight hundred and seventy-eight billion four hundred and thirty-one million, two hundred and fifty-six thousand, seven hundred and eighty-nine).

This number means something, but I've forgotten whether it's the number of creatures who have ever lived on Earth, or the number of creatures who haven't yet. Still, it's a pretty big number, isn't it? Almost big enough to account for all the atoms in, say, a medium-sized cardboard box.

Depending on what's in it.

Regardless, it has nothing whatever to do with the rest of the story, which, unfortunately, I've also forgotten.

Trailing into Nonsense

(1990)

I am
alone.
You'll say I'm just depressed—
or will you?

I don't want to scare anyone when I talk of suicide.
It isn't fear of the unknown that stops me
but love of it.

An actor, portraying my part in a movie, would do a much better job.

Part of my problem is that I live in the third person.
Do you know what it's like—
maybe you do—
to watch your every move as if it were happening to somebody else?
It makes it difficult to get too worked up about anything.
All I can do is watch myself get steadily more depressed.
I criticize myself for a poor performance.
Only when I lose myself for a moment in grief
do I congratulate myself for feeling something real.
In the act of so doing, I am once more beside myself.

I apologize for the self-pitying tone of this poem.
All I want to do is talk.
I don't want my words to be original;
I don't want my words to be beautiful;
all I want to do is talk.
So can we talk?

I'm kidding—I don't really want to talk.

I suppose Paul McCartney would say
All I need is love,
but what does Paul McCartney know?

They tell me everybody's so unique,
but I don't believe them.
We make up stories about all the things we can never do
and call it Art.
But can Art make us fly?
No, I mean literally.

When I was nine I really wanted a race car set for Christmas.
I had to get one that year because I knew that a ten-year-old would be far
     too old for one.
I had wanted it since I was five.
I wanted the Tyco® Double Looper in the Sears® *Wish Book*.
When I was ten I honestly didn't want one anymore.
If there was a point to this anecdote, I've forgotten it.

I want to fly—
I dream it, and it's a giddy,
terrifying,
momentary feeling of freedom.

The only way I would ever consider committing suicide
would be to jump out of an airplane
as high as I could without needing an oxygen mask.

At the moment before impact I would try to pull up
and fly away.

Blurred Vision

(1989)

The car window framed a streaming collage of undergrowth and telephone poles and dirt, with litter adding occasional streaks of color. The white line at the bottom swayed lazily to and fro, emphasizing everything indiscriminately. Helen wasn't exactly thinking, but against this chaotic backdrop her mind cast images of people, like in Dorothy's tornado:

Her mother, leaning close, counseling her like she would have anyone who wandered into her clinic. Rick, shifting his feet and telling her to keep the baby, that they'd run away and raise the child together. Her father, in his recliner, smoking a pipe and reading a thick novel.

When the white line, dimmed by the coming night, sank beneath its frame, the blur resolved itself into the parking lot of a gas station, and the images dropped like snow off a roof. The lack of motion outside the window did nothing to dispel her sensation of hurtling ineluctably forward.

Her car door opened, startling her, and Rick handed her a plastic bag. She hadn't even noticed him get out. The bag was filled with soda, sandwiches and candy bars.

"Supper time," said Rick, "Hey, why are you crying?"

She drew the back of her hand across one cheek. It came back wet, so she pulled a crumpled tissue out of her purse and dried her cheeks while Rick closed the door, and soon they were moving again. She ate half her sandwich and sipped some soda, but left the rest for Rick, who was grinding his food and paying too much attention to the road. She returned her attention to the blur.

At the motel, she took a long, warm shower, searching for shapes in the mildewed ceiling. Afterwards, she went to sleep like a rabbit going to ground.

She didn't fully awake the next morning until she saw cows. "I want to stop and see the cows," she said. She didn't watch his reaction as he slowly pulled over into the breakdown lane.

The cows were chewing placidly and only blinked when she stroked their noses. She breathed their rich, powerful aroma, and admired the soft, whitish-pink of their disinterested ears.

After a time, Rick asked, "Are you through talking to the cows, Hel? Can we go now?"

She half-turned toward Rick, then back to the herd. *Had she been talking to them? What had she said?* She looked at Rick again, puzzled, then walked back to the car.

Helen searched the blur for some memory of her bovine conversation. *What had she told them? What had they replied?* She wanted to go back and ask them. She turned to Rick and said, "I want . . ."

She watched him pull his bottom lip beneath his front teeth—a familiar expression.

". . . a cat." she said. She felt foolish for saying it. She didn't know what she meant by it, and Rick didn't ask, but a few minutes later they passed a hand-painted sign that said, "Free Kittens." She gasped and touched his arm. Still biting his lip, Rick blinked slowly and nodded. He pulled into the driveway and walked up to the house, leaving Helen to her thoughts, which were no less chaotic and hurtling than before. *Was he really going to come back with a cat? Why would God answer this prayer, so quickly, and none of the others, ever? Did she really want a cat? Any more than she wanted the other thing?* Rick opened her door and handed her an exceptionally large and trembly puff of milkweed that stared at her with impossibly blue eyes. So that was one question answered.

"I shall call you Fate," she said, and soon it was purring like an electric back massager.

"Fate, my dear, you're too little to sound like a truck," she said. "You must be so hungry, though, huh?" She searched the bag from yesterday's supper and pulled out the waxed paper that had held her sandwich. She scooped a dollop of tuna salad with the tip of her finger, leaving a greasy smear on the satiny surface, and offered it to the kitten, who sniffed at it timidly, waiting to see if it would hurt. Once she decided it was safe, Fate angled her head, opened her mouth, and sank her tiny fangs into the morsel.

"Mmm," said Helen, "Good tuna fish, huh?" Vicariously, she savored the texture and taste of slightly stale mayonnaise, exquisite chunks of tuna, and tiny bursts of pickle. It had tasted like nothing when she had eaten it herself.

When Fate was done licking her finger, Helen searched for more, but could find nothing to interest the kitten. After a quick cleaning, Fate crawled up onto her shoulder and explored her hair, while Helen's gaze moved once more to the window. She couldn't help speaking out when she saw another herd of cows. "Oh Fate, look! There's a horse in the middle of those cows."

"You want to go talk to it?" asked Rick, with a tired sarcasm that made her feel as small as a kitten. He pulled over without waiting for an answer and said, "Go ahead." He was trembling and red-faced, and not looking at her.

Helen frowned, but said nothing. She retrieved Fate from the fall of her hair and climbed out the door.

"Oh Fate," she sighed, hugging the warm, soft kitten to her cheek.

As she descended the small slope towards the fence, the horse walked forward to greet her. Excitement rose from her stomach at the prospect of talking to this sage beast. The beast, however, was more interested in Fate. Its muzzle gently investigated the kitten, much as Fate had investigated the tuna fish. As if she made the same connection, Fate closed her eyes, and laid her ears back flat against her head.

"You can't eat Fate, silly horse," she said. "Even if she does look rather scrumptious, hmm?" She held Fate up close to her own open mouth, close enough to taste the long silky fur.

"Don't worry, Fate, we're not going to eat you, are we horse? Of course not." She dropped Fate back to her shoulder and reluctantly glanced back at the car.

It wasn't there. She frowned and walked back up to the deserted road. Her frown took root, and she looked at Fate inquisitively. The kitten squirmed and mewled and tried to get down. She let it down and looked back at the horse, but the horse had returned to its grazing. She looked at the sky; she looked at the ground, and all around, and was amazed at how utterly still it all was. She dropped down and reclined on her side next to Fate. "I think he's gone," she said.

Fate batted a stray strand of hair and then studied it seriously, waiting for it to react.

The Return of the Queen

(2005)

Susan Ashe had lived in many places, but none of them had quite felt like home. She and her husband, Jonathan, were living in an apartment in Oak Park, Illinois when they heard that *The Chronicles of Narnia* were to be made into a movie.

"Did you read *The Guardian* this morning, dear?" asked Jonathan, tapping at the computer with one hand while he ate a bagel with the other.

Susan had been up for several hours by then (she always had been an early riser), but she had not gotten on-line yet, and she said so.

"Says here in the Arts section they're making a movie out of Narnia. It's set to be directed by the bloke what did *Shrek*."

Normally, Susan would have raised a withering eyebrow at the attempted Cockney accent, but to her husband's surprise, she made no reaction at all.

"Is something the matter, then?" As he watched her, his concern mounted, for her face was pale, her jaw clenched, and she seemed to be trembling. Alarmed, he stood up, worried she was having an attack of some kind.

What he didn't realize (because she had never told him) was that she knew more about Narnia than anyone else then living, and the place did not hold pleasant associations for her. With an effort, she got ahold of herself, looked up at Jonathan, and said, "I'm sorry. What, dear?"

"Cor. You gave me a turn there. Thought you was 'aving an embollic-kum." Jonathan had grown up in New Jersey, but once he started with the accent, he found it almost impossible to stop.

Susan took a deep breath. "Not to worry," she said. "I was just thinking about those poor children in Liberia. Really, something *ought* to be done."

Jonathan smiled, relaxing, and sat down again. Susan was always going on about some war or another. He tended to favor the Arts section over the World, but Susan would have her causes. She'd always had a tender heart toward those less fortunate. Suffering children, in particular, would get her in a rage. "Don't see what that has to do with Narnia," he said.

"I'm popping out for some coffee," she said. "Would you like something, dear?"

Jonathan greeted this with some confusion. "We've got coffee . . ." But Susan was already out the door. He gazed after her for a moment, wondering if perhaps he should follow, then shrugged and turned back to the computer. "Blimey. 'Ere I thought *I* was the loon in the fambly."

Susan reached the corner of the street before her shoulders began to shake. She crossed her arms and put her head down, fighting to keep control. It was shocking how quickly the mention of that place set her heart to beating, even after all these years. She forced her chin up, drew her arms to her sides and continued walking. The air was cool, the sidewalk still damp from the thunderstorms that had been plaguing them for days. Drops of water fell from the trees, spattering into her hair and tickling her scalp. She walked more briskly, as if she thought she could outpace them. She needed a cigarette; unfortunately, she had left them in her purse in the kitchen.

She was heading for Lake Street, which was the wrong direction for finding the solitude she desired, but having used coffee as an excuse to get out of the house, she had unthinkingly headed for Starbucks. She decided she would turn at the next corner and loop around in the other direction.

Just then, a little girl skipped down the steps of her house and started walking ahead of Susan, swinging her hair from side to side. For a moment it seemed to Susan that her heart stopped. "Lucy," she whispered. Of course she knew it wasn't her. Lucy had been dead for fifty years. Nevertheless, she didn't turn at the corner, as she had intended, but followed the little girl toward Lake Street, keeping always a few paces back. An insane part of her mind wanted to sweep the girl into her arms and kiss her and tell her she had been very naught (which had been a word of theirs) for disappearing all those years ago.

When the girl started skipping again, Susan had to quell the urge to run to keep up. She found there were tears in her eyes as she approached Lake Street, and she paused to wipe them away and touch her hair before joining the throng that was bustling to and fro. She could see no sign of the little girl.

She walked all the way to Harlem Avenue in search of her, though she couldn't have said why—she wasn't about to intrude on a little girl's errand. She crossed Lake and headed back in the other direction, thinking perhaps she *would* stop in for a cuppa (forgetting that she had forgotten her purse), but halfway there she noticed a man sitting on a bench, one arm stretched across the back of it, the other holding a cigarette. He was an older black man, who looked as if he might have spent the night on that bench, but she didn't let that bother her.

"Excuse me. Sir?" she said. The man looked up and smiled. His teeth were atrocious. "I'm sorry, I don't mean to bother you, but might you have a cigarette for a sad old lady?" She wasn't sure why she had put it like that; for one thing she wasn't so old; but there it was—there's no taking words back when once they're spoken.

"Why certainly," he said. "Have a seat next to me, sad old lady, and tell a—tell a sad old man your troubles." He handed her his crumpled pack and she fumbled one out, then handed it back to him and sat down.

"Thank you," she said, as he held up a flame. She leaned into it, then let out a long stream of smoke and sagged against the back of the bench. "Ever so much better," she said.

She glanced at the man, who was looking at her with eyes that were inscrutable but not unkind. His corneas were yellow. She took another drag. "Have you ever read *The Chronicles of Narnia?*"

"Oh, yes," he said. "The one with the ship was my favorite."

"Ahem. Yes, well, I never did. I read a good deal of *The Lion, the Witch and the Wardrobe* once in a bookstore, but . . ." She wondered, offhandedly, where she was going with this, but decided to soldier on for the moment and find out. "Em. Have you ever actually *been* to Narnia? I'm sorry: what a silly question." She laughed and tried to wave it off, but the man's inscrutable eyes never wavered. "Yes," she said. "Well, I have." A wave of emotion swept over her as she said this, a sense of release, as if a logjam had broken up on a river. She glanced quickly at him, then away. "I'm Susan Pevensie." She stopped herself from checking his reaction. "You must think I'm crazy." She looked around at all the people that were passing them. No one so much as spared them a glance. She looked at the man beside her, feeling suddenly lost.

He held out a hand to her, his face serious. "Malcolm Jones," he said.

She shook his hand. A sort of strength seemed to flow into her from that brief human contact. She took a quick drag from the cigarette, then continued. "To tell you the truth, I've spent most of my life pretending Narnia was nothing but a game. But it's not. It was real. And now there's to be a . . . a movie made of it." Again there were tears in her eyes and she brushed them brusquely away.

"The truth of it, Malcolm, the reason I've always pretended it was a game, is that . . . I miss it." The cigarette must have been stronger than the kind she was used to, for her head was feeling light. "I was heartbroken when Aslan . . ." Her mouth went tight, contorting into a trembling frown. It had been a such a long time since she had spoken that name. "I was heartbroken when He said I was never to come back. When Lucy told me about her adventures on the *Dawn Treader*, I laughed at her for being such a child, but really it was envy. I didn't want to hear about her adventures. Even when she said Aslan told her she was no longer welcome in Narnia either. . . . I *hated* her, Malcolm. I hated her for always being the one who could see him, even when the rest of us couldn't. She was always so cheerful and lighthearted. She was the sweetest little girl. Oh! I'm sorry for blubbing all over you. It's just, I thought, I thought I could go on envying her and hating her until it pleased me to stop, but then . . ." Strangely, a calm descended upon her. No tears threatened as she related the worst of it. "Then there was the train wreck, and Lucy, and all the rest. . . . I've been alone ever since." She took one more drag off her cigarette, then dropped it on the ground and stepped on it, grinding it with her toe to make sure it was out.

"Well. I feel much better now. Thank you so much for your cigarette and your listening ear." She stood up, but Malcolm put a hand to her sleeve. She looked down at him.

"Aslan still loves you, Susan."

Susan drew a deep, wavering breath and pulled away. "Yes, well, he has a peculiar way of showing it."

She walked away, feeling like she was swimming, like her legs didn't want to obey. Before she had gotten very far, she found she was shaking uncontrollably. Panicked, she ducked into an alley, her eyes closed tight against the tears, her fists balled as if in rage. She stumbled forward, trying to get as deeply into the alley as she could before she lost control completely. At last she could go no further, and leaned against the wall, giving full rein to her sobs.

After a bit she noticed something strange about the texture of the wall and opened her eyes. She was leaning against the rough bark of a tree and there was grass beneath her feet. She looked up at the tree, the sweep of her gaze taking in a long downhill descent, a tiny beach, and the distant ocean.

"At last," said the tree. "You've come at last."

Susan stepped back. The tree was actually a giant woman. What she had been leaning against was the woman's leg. She was unmistakably the dryad of a Narnian willow tree, stout with age, but graceful still, with long flowing hair that brushed against Susan's own. She looked as old as Susan felt, and of course, even with her smile she seemed unutterable sad.

"You—you've been expecting me?"

"Yes," she said softly, in a dreamy sort of voice, "I knew you'd come eventually. Coriakin said you mightn't, but I never doubted you, and I've never stopped asking Aslan."

"Aslan?" said Susan. "Is he here?" She looked around as though she fully expected to see the gigantic golden lion standing nearby.

"Oh, no. No, your highness. I've not seen him since he gave Speech to the mice, and asked us to look after them especially. But he speaks to me sometimes, and I talk to him almost constantly."

Susan blushed at being called *Your highness*, and said, "Please, dear Willow, I'm just plain Susan now. I haven't been queen for a great many years."

"Once a Queen in Narnia, always a Queen in Narnia. A thousand years can't change that."

Susan frowned. "A thousand . . . ?"

The willow cast her eyes up and seemed to be counting on her fingers. "One thousand, two hundred and ninety-four. Or is it ninety-six?" She gazed at Susan sadly. "You don't remember me, do you?"

"Remember?"

"Oh, I did think you'd remember. I suppose I've changed a lot more than you have. Why, you hardly seem to have aged at all! And here I am, a whole millennium older than when I raced you and the *Splendor Hyaline*, and I look every bit of it, I'm sure."

Susan gaped, nonplussed, but slowly her memories clicked into place, and she let out a gasp. "O-o-oh! You're Cymbeline." Susan sat down. Her legs just seemed to crumple beneath her, as memories flooded back of the young willow tree who had been her best friend at Cair Paravel. "We thought, I thought I had lost you. We searched all over Avra. I . . . ." Her eyes moved back and forth as though she were reading a book, remembering the details. She couldn't bear to meet the tree's eyes. "You went further, didn't you? You said you'd race me to the farthest isle."

"Yes. I thought I was such a wonderful swimmer. I told you no boat made of dead wood could beat a living tree for swimming. I didn't even stop at Avra. I just swam right past it, thinking how surprised you would be."

A weight of guilt overwhelmed Susan. This was why she hated thinking about Narnia. There was so much guilt here, and people were always expecting far too much of her. She glared at Cymbeline, her anger mounting. Cymbeline was still gazing into the distance with sad, dreamy eyes. Susan's anger softened, but her guilt remained. She said, "Lucy wanted to go farther. Lucy and that beastly mouse. You remember: Queekle. The First Mouse."

Cymbeline's eyes lit up. "Yes! I remember Queekle. How is he these days?"

Susan stared at her, suddenly exasperated. "No, you don't understand. I, I left you out there. Lucy *said* you might be farther along, and Queekle insisted it was a matter of honor that we find you, dead or alive, but I assured everyone that you would come back on your own if we didn't meet you, and it was getting late in the year, and Peter agreed with me, saying we daren't leave Narnia ungoverned for too long, and . . . Oh, Cymbeline! I've been saying no to Aslan my whole life. I've been awful! For years I've been catching sight of Lucy, and feeling that, if I only followed after her, we'd meet again in Narnia, and always I've told myself not to think nonsense: Lucy is dead, and Narnia never existed. Only now, when I finally have followed her, or someone who reminded me of her, and I really do come to Narnia, I find you here instead of Lucy, and you've been waiting all this time, and it's all my fault, as usual, and I don't want any of it, do you hear me? I just want to go home!"

"There, there," said Cymbeline, smoothing Susan's hair with her long fingers.

"I'm a grown woman! I'm too old for these childish games!"

"Your highness, you look like a child to me."

"I know, to you, I look like a child, but really I'm quite old for a . . ." Susan looked at her hands. They were smaller than they should be, and not as bony. She put her hands to her face, and felt skin that was supple and without any wrinkles that she could feel. The truth finally dawned on her. "Why, so I am a child!"

For a moment she forgot all her rage and guilt, and whooped for joy. Then she looked into Cymbeline's eyes, really gazed into them. She was surprised and touched by what she saw there. Tension left her body as if a sluice had been opened in her chest. "I am sorry, my dearest Cymbeline. Can you ever forgive me?"

Cymbeline closed her eyes, and a huge, shining tear fell from both eyelids. "There's nothing to forgive, my dear Queen: You're here. You must admit, though, I won the race by quite a long margin."

Susan laughed. And to hear the sound of her childhood voice in laughter was more than she could stand. Had there been any laughter since she last left Narnia?

Together, she and Cymbeline laughed and wept, and embraced each other fiercely, until they were once more as they had been a thousand years ago: the very best of friends.

When at last they were still, Susan asked, "But why didn't you swim back, Cymbel? You must have known, after winter, at least, that we wouldn't be coming."

"Yes, well, there was the dragon, you see."

"Oh, Cymbel, a dragon! How terrifying!"

"Well, no. Not really. You may not know it, your highness, but on land, a tree is more than a match for a dragon. We're both magical creatures, you see. Now, when I arrived . . . Oh dear, I remember it like it was yesterday, swimming in the ocean, exhausted, with no earth to draw strength from. I was really quite defenseless. When it saw me it attacked me at once, and there was nothing I could do but roll in the water to keep the flames from catching. You've no idea how tired I was, but I managed to make landfall in the end, and then I was able to unleash some fireworks of my own. Anyway, I've been waiting for you to arrive so we can kill it. For only a knight, a son of Adam or a daughter of Eve, can kill a dragon."

"Oh dear," said Susan. "I should have guessed there was a reason Aslan wanted me here. I suppose, if I hadn't been so beastly on the *Splendor Hyaline*, Peter and Edmund and Queekle could have taken care of it. Now it's just you and me, and I can't think how I can find the courage to face it."

"It's worse than you think, I'm afraid," said Cymbeline, sadly.

"Worse? What could be worse than a dragon?"

Cymbeline's face clouded. "It's just, you see, I've been waiting so long, and . . ."

"What is it? Oh, dearest Cymbeline, don't spare my feelings, just tell me what worse damage I've caused."

Cymbeline was silent for a long while, staring at Susan with her sad eyes, her sad smile. "Willows aren't supposed to live a thousand years, my young Queen."

Susan's eyes widened. "You don't mean—Oh no!" They were both crying again, hugging each other as hard as they could. "How long?" asked Susan, plaintively.

"Not long, I'm afraid. And we still need to build you a coracle. Have you ever built a coracle, my dear?"

"A what-acle?"

Cymbeline drew her hands through her hair, pulling out long wands of willow until there was a large pile at her feet. "There," she said. "That ought to do for the frame. As for the rest, well, let's see, somewhere in here I have a sail-making kit. . . ." To Susan's horror, Cymbeline had opened up a crack in her torso, which suddenly looked a lot more trunk-like than it had a moment ago. She was hollow inside, and the hollow seemed to be crammed with all manner of trinkets and baubles and clutter. She dug around for several minutes before she pulled out a largish wooden box. "Here it is!" she cried, and opened it. Inside was a folded piece of canvas, a ball of twine, a large pair of scissors, a bottle of resin and several triangular needles. "This should do wonderfully. One of the Narnian Lords who stopped by not long ago left this with me. Just in the nick of time, too! They were very sympathetic about the dragon, but had no wish to face it themselves. It seems they were already on the run from some tyrant or other. Oh, this is so much fun!"

Over the next several days, Cymbeline taught Susan how to build a coracle, using the willow wands as a frame. They talked about their memories of Cair Paravel, and Susan tried to tell her about life in America, but it was all too foreign and strange for Cymbeline really to understand. Once they finished the boat, Cymbel pointed out the island she was to row towards and what stars she should follow during the night, so that she could travel southeast in more or less of a straight line. Then they carefully descended the mountain to the beach and Cymbeline gave her lessons on how to paddle it (you paddle in the bow, using a sort of figure-eight stroke). Whenever Susan asked what she was to do when she got there, all the old Willow would say is, "There's a lovely little village there, where the villagers are lost and lonely and afraid. You must encourage them." But why they needed encouragement, she would not say.

At last Cymbel said it was time for her to go.

"I don't want to go," said Susan. A tear welled up in her eye and slid down her cheek. The old Willow reached down and picked her up, cradling her in her arms.

"There, there," she said. "Don't be sad. We may yet meet again, you and I. It was good of you to come. I wish we could have spent more time together. But don't worry: Time won't last forever. Commend yourself to Aslan and set out. That's half the battle, you know, just setting out. Trust Aslan to see to the other half." The old tree smiled and set Susan down. "Good-bye, Queen Susan," she said. Susan simply stood, her hands to her sides, unable to speak.

Cymbeline closed her eyes and her womanly form faded away, and she was just a willow tree, out of place on the beach, and one last leaf fell from her branches.

Susan lay down at her feet for a few hours, weeping a little and sleeping a little. She considered abandoning the adventure, but she had nowhere to go, and the dragon would discover that Cymbeline was dead before too long. It would be best to be with other people when that happened, so she pushed the coracle into the water and stepped into it.

For three days she tossed on the gentle waves, paddling as much as she was able, sleeping at times, at other times just gazing at the stars. The weather those three days was warm and gentle, and not at all like any other time she had been at sea.

It occurred to her that she had never really been alone before, in all her life. She had, perhaps, avoided any opportunities for it. But now that she had no choice, she found she didn't mind it so much. The loneliness seeped into her bones and the beauty and grandeur of the endless waves, sunrise and sunset, the large, almost intimate stars seeped in as well, until she was saturated with a peace she had never dreamed of. Fortunately she didn't remember (for she hadn't been paying close attention when Lucy told her) that these waters were very near the place the *Dawn Treader* had been attacked by the sea serpent. When her boat touched ground, she was almost sad to leave it.

It was early morning when she landed, and a few villagers were out fishing. Most of them withdrew back to their huts upon sight of her, but one young woman, whose name (she would later learn) was Margaret, seeing that Susan was only (as she appeared) a little girl, walked up to her and asked her from whence she had come. Susan looked back over the water and pointed vaguely. She couldn't quite make out Cymbeline's island. Margaret decided she had been shipwrecked, as everyone knew that the only island to the west was inhabited by demons, and this quickly became the consensus in the village.

It was amazing to Susan (when she stopped to think about it, which wasn't often) how quickly she was accepted into the community. Margaret's husband, James, welcomed her into their home as though he suddenly had five children instead of four. She learned to do chores with the other girls and no one questioned her further about the circumstances of her arrival. When Susan asked how the villagers had come to settle on the island, they were divided in their opinions. Some said they were ancestors of the Telmarines, a shipload of whom had landed some years ago. Others (mostly the younger ones) told a story of how their ancestors had come through a door in a tree hundreds of years ago. Others believed they'd always been there. Susan couldn't quite place their accent, but it didn't sound like Caspian's. She thought it might be American, perhaps from the northeast.

On Sundays they went to church. The church was the only wooden building in the village, as there were few trees on the island. There were no prayer books or hymnals, but they had one antique Bible, and their service, as far as Susan could tell, was not so different from the Anglican services she had grown up with, only distorted, as one would expect after generations without access to a Prayer Book.

As an adult, Susan had rarely gone to church except to accompany her husband at Christmas and Easter, and then only under duress. It was different now. She was back in Narnia; she was a child again. She enjoyed sitting in the pews surrounded by her adoptive family. Miracles were possible. She listened to the vicar's sermons eagerly, wondering what Christians thought about miracles, it being a word of theirs.

To her disappointment, the sermons were more about how God rewarded hard work and simple living. As far as Susan could tell, everyone was taking that advice. She began to wonder, though, if they needed to be told every week. She began to sense a pervasive sadness in the community. Everyone had a routine, and Susan enjoyed the routine immensely, but she began to wonder if there wasn't a spark missing. Something to give their lives meaning and purpose.

After she had been there for almost a year, Susan asked Margaret why no one ever spoke of Aslan.

"Who's Aslan, then?" asked Margaret.

By now Susan was used to such responses when it came to modern things from America, but she was always taken aback by how ignorant these people were about all things Narnian. They had stories about talking animals and walking trees, but knew nothing about which direction Narnia lay or any of its history. But to have lived here for generations, hundreds of years, it seemed, and never to have heard of or been visited by Aslan; Susan couldn't understand it.

From that day forward her happiest times would be telling the family stories about Narnia by the fireside every night. All about the castle at Cair Paravel, the feasts and the clothes, their adventures at sea, their travels to Calormen, about the animals and the trees and the river gods and goddesses.

As the weeks went by, neighbors started stopping by to listen, so that the little house at which she was staying became quite crowded. Susan was surprised by how much she remembered from when she was a Queen in Narnia so long ago. At first she had tried to gloss over her station, for fear that people would think she thought too highly of herself, or start treating her differently, but there was no escaping such facts as the stories poured from her heart. There was a passion there that she hardly would have believed she possessed. Whether people believed her stories or not, no one ever questioned her, nor, to her unending relief, did they treat her any differently, though some of the children got to calling her Queen Susan. She found she didn't mind.

It was a long time before she could bring herself to say much about Aslan, though the children clamored for her to tell them more about the lion. "Was he a *scary* lion?" they asked. "Yes," she answered, thinking, *but not in the way you imagine*. Susan had been afraid of Aslan her whole life. As she told those old, old stories, she began to remember that it hadn't always been that way. Once upon a time, the name of Aslan had thrilled her beyond measure, and that was before she had even met him. What had happened since then?

When the villagers asked her to move her storytelling to the chapel, so that more people could attend, she decided she would start again, from the beginning this time, and tell the whole story. At first, she found it more difficult to tell her stories there. It was a less comfortable surrounding, and she found herself telling the story as she remembered it from Lewis's book that one time in the bookshop, rather than from her own memories of being there. Nevertheless, as time went on she grew more comfortable, and her memories became clearer.

She sat on the steps before the altar, and the children gathered around her in the aisle gazing wide-eyed, while the grownups sat in the pews, more difficult to see in the dim light of candles. She felt like some old wise-woman in a tepee in ancient America, passing down legends to her tribe. The children gasped when she told them the Witch had made it winter in Narnia, "winter, but never Christmas." It thrilled her in a way she never remembered feeling when she spoke to her own children, or her grandchildren. It was like she was becoming a new person, or perhaps like becoming her old self again, and that reminded her of how Lucy used to tell the story of Edmund after Aslan saved him, that "He was his old self again, and could look you in the eye." As she got closer to the climax of that story, she found she would have to stop at times, for fear that her voice would betray the tears she felt rising. Each time she paused the silence would fill the nave, while everyone waited patiently for her to continue.

The vicar in particular would express his appreciation for her stories. "You tell them as though you actually believed them," he said, and he said it as though he were paying a high and earnest compliment. She didn't argue the point.

At last, one chill, Autumn night, she came to the part when she and Lucy had been unable to sleep and had gone looking for Aslan. As she told of how sad he was, and how she and her sister had walked beside him with their hands in his mane, his scent seemed to rise about her again, pungent and wild and warm—so real that she looked about—but he wasn't there: just his fragrance. She couldn't tell if anyone else could smell it, and she never asked, but afterwards people said she fairly glowed as she spoke.

She ended the story that night with Aslan's death. For the first time, people left the chapel in silence. There were tears in the eyes of some of the children, but they asked no questions. Susan wanted to tell them it was all right, to comfort them that he had come back to life, that his mane had grown back, that the mice had not gnawed through his cords in vain, but she was too sad herself to continue. He had died. Aslan, the great Lion, the hope of Narnia, had been tortured and killed so that Edmund, dead these many years, could live a little longer. Her brother. Her dear brother. She sat in the chapel alone after everyone else left. She wondered if now, at last, Aslan might show himself.

Once the thought entered her head, she found she couldn't leave. For the first time since she had arrived, she *wanted* him to show up, to convince her with his presence that he was not dead. She had been afraid, up until then, that he would show up and give her some task to accomplish, some rescue to affect, that he would tell her to hurry up and slay the dragon so she could go back, back to the husband she cared for, yes, but, to the world she loved? No.

She would not have thought she could stay there all night, sitting on the steps of the sanctuary, but time passed, and at length the darkness eased. *Now*, she thought. *Now he will come.* She waited till the first rays of dawn touched the east-facing windows. *Now*, she thought. *Now.* But he did not come. With a heavy heart, she stirred herself at last and thought of her bed of heather. She rose and stretched, staring at the cross silhouetted against the bright window.

A noise from behind distracted her. She turned. James was entering the nave, followed by the rest of his family. They spoke not a word, but sat in their accustomed seats. They seemed not the least surprised to find her there. They looked, in fact, hollow-eyed and slow, as if they, too, had watched through the night. Soon others joined them. Within the hour, it seemed the entire village was there, all silent, all waiting. So far, no one had met her eyes, but all seemed lost in thought. The children sat with their parents. It occurred to Susan that it was Sunday morning, but too early for the service. Then she noticed, in the very back, the vicar, sitting alone, a look of intense concentration on his face.

Susan turned to the cross behind her, gazing up at it. She found, for the first time in months, that she wanted a cigarette. At last she turned back to the congregation, her family, and lifted her hands. All eyes lifted to hers. She spoke, but the words seemed hardly her own:

"Rejoice, my people. Lift up your eyes. Cast off your sorrow. The night indeed is ended, and the day has come at last. The light has shone in the darkness, and the darkness has not overcome it."

While she spoke, a gigantic golden lion entered the chapel.

Susan dropped to her knees. "Oh, Aslan!" she cried. The lion paced up the aisle. A rustling and creaking accompanied him, as the villagers, too, went to their knees as he passed. She didn't know how she could look at him steadily, but she dared not drop her eyes, for fear that he would be gone. Halfway to the altar he turned into a man. He stepped up into the sanctuary and placed his hand on her head. "Well met, my beloved." Susan burst out with a sob that seemed to rip her heart in two.

The man looked up at the cross and smiled, as though acknowledging an old friend. Then he turned and faced the congregation. "Alleluia! I am risen!"

As one the villagers responded. "You are risen indeed. Alleluia!"

In that tiny village, on an unnamed island in a world that some consider make-believe, the church experienced what all churches have longed for since the beginning. The Lord of Light, the Son of the Emperor-over-the-Sea, Jesus himself, led the service. I cannot begin to describe what communion was like that day. Susan received first, then helped him serve the others.

When the service was over, Jesus shook hands with each one of them at the door, and as they mingled around outside, they laughed, for each of their faces was glowing, and they thought their hearts would burst with joy and wonder.

Inside the church, Susan looked stricken. "Oh, Aslan, no!" she cried.

The man who no longer looked like a lion cupped his hand around Susan's neck and gazed at her with eyes that still resembled Aslan's.

Susan wrenched away and crossed her arms over her chest. "Why do you let these things happen? Do you *like* to watch people die? There are children out there! *Children!* Do you really intend to stand by and do nothing while a dragon comes and eats them?"

"Peace, child," he said, but Susan would not be calmed.

"Everything I've ever had you've taken away from me! First Narnia, then Lucy, my whole family, now this! If you hate me so much, why don't you just kill *me?*" Her hands were at her sides, now, fists balled, spittle flying from her mouth as she screamed, her face white and twisted with rage. The story she had just finished telling seemed suddenly foolish and false.

"It is necessary for the happy ending I have planned."

"What does *that* mean?"

"It means that the story I am telling, and the war that I am waging, are more complicated and dire than you can imagine. The dragon is coming, was coming whether the people here were prepared or not. Because of you, because they listened to the stories you told and believed in them, they were prepared to receive my blessing. They have been sanctified. Once the dragon destroys this town and eats his fill of these people you have loved, he will grow very ill. In three years' time he will die. His death in this manner, at that time, is crucial. It is for this reason that I have bent my own rules to bring you here. In a few moments you will hear a familiar sound and return to your own place. I charge you to remember all the things that have happened here, so that these people may have a witness and so that you may learn to understand and accept that my ways are never cruel or capricious. Read the Chronicles of Narnia. Strive to understand the story of these people in the light of what is to come. Even now Prince Caspian is engaging his uncle's troops in battle. He is putting your horn to his lips. Do you hear it? Strive to understand, and do not lose heart. I have loved you well and will never leave you or forsake you. Go in peace, my beloved Susan."

As he spoke these last words, his voice grew faint, and Susan felt herself being pulled or tugged straight out of the world. In a moment she was back in the alley in Oak Park, leaning against the wall, and she could not tell if the tears on her cheeks were the one's she had shed before she left, or if they were new. She wiped them away and walked back toward the street.

Malcolm was sitting on the bench, as before. They stared at each other in silence while people streamed past between them. He lifted his pack of cigarettes. Susan sat down beside him and accepted his offer.

"Thank you," she said.

"Thank *you*," said Malcolm.

Nuts

(1997?)

I was running late,
as usual,
so I cut through the park to save time.
There were leaves on the path,
and I wondered,
irritated,
when the grounds crew would get around
to raking them up, for
they made a hideous racket.

Something small
and hard struck my temple. I stopped
abruptly,
but turned slowly,
the better to glower at the culprit,
but there was no one there but a tree.
I lifted my glare to the branches and caught sight of
a squirrel
in the act
of throwing another acorn at my head.

I caught it, deftly,
and contemplated chucking it back, but
something in the way the squirrel had tossed it
underhand
reminded me of a senior citizen
feeding pigeons or throwing snacks to a dog.
Nonplussed,

I popped the nut into my mouth and
bit down.
It wasn't very good, so
I waited until the squirrel wasn't looking,
then spit it out—I didn't want to seem ungrateful.

Beyond the tree was the same old lake,
shimmering in the early morning sun, surrounded
by the same old naked trees, but
there was something odd—
in the middle of the lake was a
hole.
I was snaking my head around to adjust my perspective, when
a bit of smoke curled out, along with a couple of sparks.
A group of children dressed in clothes that were far too big for them
swarmed across the surface of the lake like
windblown leaves,
lay down on their stomachs
at the edge of the hole and
peered inside.
One of them shouted that it was just a group of frogs
sitting around a campfire grilling trout.

Curious to see this wonder for myself
(but unwilling to trust my weight to surface tension), I
grabbed the lowest limb of the squirrel's tree
and yanked myself up. With no little difficulty,
I managed to scooch a ways out
onto a high, thick branch
overhanging the water, but
the hole was too deep for me to glimpse its bottom.

An odd cooing sound, louder than any pigeon,
startled me,
and I cautiously glanced behind.
No source could I find,
but the branch on which I sat
began to bounce.
Terrified,
I wrapped my arms and legs around it.
The bouncing and cooing continued until,
if you can believe it, I started to cry.

Immediately,
the eerie noise and motion ceased, but
my bawling did not, for two higher branches
were descending upon me,
grasping me by the waist and lifting me up.
I was wailing now,
wordlessly,
screaming for help
as the nightmarish branches
deposited me firm
against the trunk of a neighboring tree,
whose bark was not so rough
or cold, and
whose branches held me gently in place.
A dozen or so twigs tapped softly upon my back,
while the squirrel
played peek-a-boo
from the other side of the trunk until
slowly, my sobbing subsided.

Below me, the children with oversized clothing
were gathering to watch.
The tree that now held me made
shushing sounds
and patted their heads with its lowermost branches.

Though its bark was making a
deep
impression in my cheeks,
eventually I fell asleep.

When I awoke, my clothes were far too big for me.

Who Is for Hallelujah

(1996)

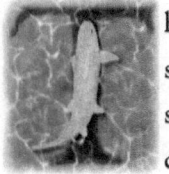he mottled, speckled brook trout hangs silent in the clear, shallow stream. The sandy bottom, strewn with pebbles and scattered about with larger stones, blends with the fish, conspiring to keep it alive. Undeterred, the osprey continues to drop from the sky. Her wings snap out like sheets as her talons skewer trout. For an extended moment she furiously flaps, clutching at the slippery wind, till at last she pulls her prey from its pool. She glides upriver, intent on her nest. The stream continues its conspiracy, seemingly unaware that it has failed.

Steve Holt rests his hand on the cold bark of a tree and fills his lungs with chilling air, then exhales, watching his breath curl in upon itself among the snow. Before him, Sarah hops lightly but stiffly from one shard of granite to another. Around him, beech trees lean at slight angles, as if they had once tried to walk. Steve takes another breath and continues downhill, leaping heavily from granite to granite.

Within the clouds, a host of angels practice Handel's *Hallelujah Chorus*, dancing among snowflakes.

"Makes you think of Christmas, doesn't it?" says Steve.

"What does?" asks Sarah.

"The snow, the clouds. I keep hearing the Hallelujah Chorus."

"That's because I keep singing it."

"Makes you think of Christmas, doesn't it?"

Sarah laughs and leans her head against his shoulder.

Steve puts his arm around her and squeezes. "What say we set up camp?"

"Already? But it's not even dark yet." She puts on her deep, mock-Steve voice: "If this were the Paleolithic Age we wouldn't even consider pitching a tent until at least 7:30."

"Very funny."

Shrugging off their packs, they sit down on the bank of a stream, with their backs against a rock, and barter bread and cheese. Their canteens dribble cold, treated water down their chins and onto their coats.

Sarah nuzzles the arm of Steve's parka, then leans back, grimacing, and swipes at the film of mucous left by her nose. She smiles sheepishly, making a face of it, her eyes slightly crossed. Steve raises an eyebrow.

"Okay!" says Sarah, jumping to her feet. "I'll go get some firewood."

Steve wastes a few seconds pulling at his parka's shoulder, trying to see what's there, then stands up and begins to drag the side of his boot through crusted leaves, baring ground for a fire. Rocks no bigger than curled-up cats lie scattered, just the right size for a firepit. While he's arranging them in a lopsided circle, Sarah returns, drops two handfuls of birch bark into the middle of the circle, then wanders off again. When the firepit is complete, Steve pulls a faded green pup tent out of his pack and sets it up, pounding the stakes into the ground with a rock, while Sarah brings twigs, branches and fallen tree limbs.

Leaning into his carefully constructed pyre, Steve fumbles with a match, gripping it by sight with numbed fingers. He inhales too much sulfur when it's struck, and coughs. The flame caresses the birch bark and spreads like syrup. He leans back, satisfied.

Trying to snuggle but distanced by their coats, they wait for the fire to roar.

"Come on," Sarah quavers, conducting the flames higher with her mittened hands.

"Gosh, it's cold," says Steve.

The osprey in her nest glares down at the river. Her head sinks into her shoulders, and she refuses to blink. Snowflakes stick to her beak, but she ignores them, focusing her rage on the river. She doesn't remember why she's so angry, but with the last of the daylight, her eyes grow large, and at last she understands. Hugging herself against the cold, she drifts like the snow towards sleep. She hiccups briefly, tasting fish.

Sarah gazes at the blank horizon and imagines the unseen sunset is reflected in her irises. She breathes in the oranges and blues that are sadly lacking from the sky and puffs out fire-illumined mist. The sharpened, white-tipped stick in her hand yearns for another marshmallow. Reaching her hand into the sticky bag, she pulls one out, impales it, and lowers it into the fire. When it catches, she brings it close to her face to feel the heat, then blows it out and eats it. The crunchy, sooty shell collapses onto a middle that is gooey on the outside, cool and marshmallowy at its core. She pulls the stick through her teeth and murmurs, "Mmmm."

"Can I have a marshmallow?" asks Steve.

Sarah pouts and considers.

He tries his manly voice: "Give me a marshmallow, woman!"

Sarah glowers.

"Please?"

She swings the bag into his chest and lets it drop.

"Thank you," he says, in a smallish voice.

He skewers three marshmallows and lowers them over some of the cooler embers. He balances the stick on a rock, occasionally twisting it until the marshmallows are lightly and evenly browned. He pulls them off with his fingers and pops them into his mouth. When the third one is finished, he closes his eyes and leans his head against Sarah's shoulder.

An owl alights on a rock on the other side of the fire. Sarah nudges Steve.

"I've been watching you eat," says the owl.

Steve and Sarah glance at each other moving only their eyes. For a moment they consider dismissing the words, but the authority in the owl's rich, woodwind voice brooks no doubt of its reality. They huddle closer, like five-day-old kittens, watching the owl with awe-widened eyes.

The owl leans forward to look at the ground, like a stout lecturer pondering his next line of thought, but it turns out he's just being shy. "Might I have a marshmallow?" he asks.

The bag is still in Steve's lap. He looks at it, then up at the owl. He utters a brief, bewildered, guttural laugh.

"If it's a problem," says the owl, hurriedly, "if you don't have enough . . . I understand."

"N-no! It's . . . Here!" He reaches into the bag with fingers once more numb, and somehow pulls out a marshmallow. He holds out his hand and begins to stand up, but the owl waves his wing to stop him.

"Just toss it," he says.

Steve's hand jerks, and he flings the marshmallow well past the owl.

There is an awkward pause.

Slowly the owl twists his neck around to see where it's landed. With remarkable dexterity, he walks backward until the marshmallow is in front of him. His neck swivels forward and he reaches down to pick it up in his beak. Then he walks back to the stone. He spares not a glance at either of them, but leans his head back as if taking in the stature of a giant. He opens his beak wider and gives a quick jerk to shake the marshmallow off the tip of his beak. He swallows it whole with a shudder, then looks at them and closes his eyes. "Mmmmmmarvelous."

Steve looks at him suspiciously. "How can you say 'Mmmm' without any lips?"

The owl's eyes snap open. "What an odd question! Of all the things to ask a talking owl!"

"Sorry," says Steve, meekly but still on guard.

"You've gotten my feathers all ruffled."

The owl suddenly grows twice as big, ruffling all his feathers. When he subsides, not a feather is out of place. The scene grows dim, the fire begins to swirl. A slow, lugubrious voice says, "Watch your wife."

Steve puts his arm around Sarah's shoulders and says "Sarah!" sharply. The fire unswirls and the scene settles back into place. An owl still stands on a rock across the fire, watching her with a worried expression. She stares at it for a long time, her eyes retreating under her brow in perplexity and worry. "What's your name?" she says at last.

The owl seems to brighten. "Now, that's more like it. My name . . ." he pauses for effect, "is up to you. Please, though, neither Wol nor Archimedes. Use your imaginations."

Steve and Sarah exchange another glance. The silence begins to stretch.

The owl seems to pose, waiting for his name.

Steve says, "Hallelujah."

The owl leaps backward as though burnt. "How did—Oh my!" He hops jerkily, turning to the right and left as if in panic. At last he settles down and stares at the sky as if beseeching it for an answer. "Well. Yes," he says. "I suppose the fairies told you." He looks at them, cocking his head slightly, like a substitute teacher who is not amused. After another awkward pause he says, "Would you like to hear a story?"

"Yes!" says Sarah, as though she has been waiting for the owl to ask.

"Very well, then. Listen, then, to the story of 'How the Osprey Lost Her Mind.'" The owl takes a deep breath, which quivers somewhat at the end. "Emma was a househuman, married to an officehuman, who decided to leave her house for awhile and take a hike. She got as far as this very river and, tragically, fell in. Now, this Emma had been having a miserable day, and falling into a river was the proverbial last straw. There may have been screaming. She certainly stood up and jumped, stomping on the river with both feet. Finally, she cursed the river as horribly as she knew how, kicking great sprays of water in every direction.

"Now, as you may know, you can curse at many deities all day long and suffer no worse than a bent feather, or a crick in one's neck, but rivers are . . . well . . . fluid. This river leaped up in front of her and cursed her right back.

"Not the transformational sort of curse, you understand, but just a spiteful invective against househumans who should never have left their kitchens.

"Emma was so astonished and terrified that she wanted to jump out of the water and not come down, but with the banks too far away, and without the use of any wings, she chose instead to stand stock still, as if the water had frozen around her knees. Mustering up a grain of courage, she apologized, if haughtily.

'Well I'm sorry,' she said. 'I suppose it wasn't entirely your fault, but really, those stones are very treacherous, and I'm sure you're responsible for that. Still, if the sun hadn't been so damnably dazzling, I might have made it across just fine. So . . .' She wagged her shoulders and glanced around for more courage. 'If you'll take back what you said about my kitchen, I'll take back what I said about you, and we'll call it even.'"

"Brave woman," said Sarah.

"Really," said Steve.

"Hmph," said Hallelujah. "That remains to be seen. The sun, you see, had something to say in his defense.

"'I say,' said the sun, 'I don't see why I should be blamed. If it wasn't for me, you wouldn't have seen the river was there in the first place. Besides, I was only trying to make things a little prettier.'

"Emma was even more astonished at being addressed by the sun, though of course, she had no trouble identifying the source of the voice. The sun sounds like a crystal tuning fork pitched almost too high—"

"Hang on a second," says Steve. "I happen to know that it takes eight minutes for sunlight to reach the earth, and that nothing travels faster than light, so if you're trying to tell us that—"

"Steve," says Sarah, making two syllables of it.

"No, no," says the owl, "it's a fair question." His eyes drill into Steve's and there is another awkward pause. "Think of it this way. The sun is a nearly infinite being, whose consciousness extends as far as his rays. That consciousness is omnipresent within that span, so that there is no need for thoughts to 'travel' from one part of the sun to another. At night, with cloud cover, it's true, the sun is only barely present, but that doesn't mean he's not aware of what's going on. He could be if he wanted to." Hallelujah pauses, peering around as if fearing to be overheard. Softly, he says, "I personally believe he . . . the sun . . . had something of a crush on Emma. From all reports, he was shining with particular brilliance that day, possibly in an attempt to impress her."

Hallelujah cleared his throat and continued in a normal tone of voice. "Emma, as I was saying, was even more astonished at being addressed by the sun. She was sorry she had tried to be brave before, for now all she wanted to do was disappear. The problem, of course, which she intuitively grasped, is that there is nowhere (outside of a house) to hide from the sun. She had only two choices. She could faint dead away or get very, very angry. She thought of her own safe kitchen not so far away, and to her surprise, she found her temples beginning to throb.

"'A pox upon you both!' she screamed, straining her voice with angry fear. 'Clouds,' she commanded, 'obscure the sun but give no rain to the river for seven months!' Her arms were stretched toward the sky, and her legs were braced apart. She looked a little like a deity herself just then.

"The sun and the river looked at each other, embarrassed, despite themselves, at how unimpressed they were by her curse. 'Look,' said the sun, 'I don't mean to sound self-important, but really, I wouldn't mind at all if the earth were covered up with clouds; it's prettier that way.'

"'I'm spring-fed,' said the river, almost apologetically.

"'All right then,' said Emma, rubbing her hands together. 'May your hydrogen turn to lead. May you turn into nothing but a big black hole!' Her head was thrust forward, chin out. It was clear she meant business.

"The sun blanched a little in spite of itself. 'I say,' it said, 'that hardly seems fair. I was only . . . trying to help.'

"The river laughed meanly. 'Not letting a little housewench scare you, are you? Big bad star like you? Letting a human being get under your skin? Ha ha ha.'

"'As for you,' said Emma, with a restraint that was awesome to behold, 'May the filth of a thousand toilets back into your waterways and choke you!'

"The river wailed and fell to his knees, so that the great sun laughed in spite of himself. The river lowered its eyebrows and began to pant. 'For that,' it said, 'I'm going to turn you into a willow tree, so that you have to drink my water, no matter what happens to it.'

"'Look here,' said the sun, who has always been big-hearted. 'You don't have to—' but it was no use: he could tell that the river was deadly serious. 'Not a tree, anyway. Something more mobile, less rigid than a tree.'

"'How about a snake?' said the river. 'A river snake, so that she has to swim around in all that kaka.'

"'No,' said the sun, like a mother trying to get her toddler to share. 'It's okay to make her something that needs to be by a river, but it doesn't have to be something horrible. Her curse probably won't come true anyway. How about a bird? An osprey maybe.'

"Emma's face was turning purple with rage. 'Let me go!' she screamed, though, in truth, no one was holding her. 'I don't want to be turned into anything!'

"'All right then,' said the river. 'An osprey.'

"'Okay,' said the sun, 'but just so you don't go and do something worse to her when this part of the world turns away from me, the spell goes off at night. She'll be asleep and immune from all spells until dawn. Agreed?'

"'Fine,' said the river, begrudgingly. He turned to Emma with something like glee in his eyes and slowly raised his arms above his head, bits of electricity buzzing about his hands.

"'Walk to the bank, dear,' the sun said, kindly.

"Emma's anger had evaporated. She tore her gaze from the river's arms and waded quickly to the steep bank and scrambled up. Sensibly enough, she tried to run, but her legs were too stiff and short for running, and her knees were bending in the wrong direction. She tripped, flung out her hands to catch herself, and took for a moment to the air. She tried to cry out but only squawked. She had turned into an osprey.

"That, of course, was when she lost her mind."

"Whew," says Steve and Sarah together, shaking their heads in unison.

"Still," says Steve, "I don't see—"

"Steve!" says Sarah, disapprovingly.

Steve looks hard at the owl. "Where is she? Now, I mean."

"In a tree not far from here. Would you like to see?"

"No," says Sarah quickly.

Steve half smiles, still looking hard at the owl. "Yeah. I think I would."

"Follow me," says Hallelujah, jumping into the air.

"Come on," says Steve, grabbing Sarah's hand.

She tries to resist, but the thought of staying behind alone is unbearable, so she lets Steve pull her into a slow run, and they follow the barely visible owl. They travel uphill beside the river until their legs are burning and their chests are tight. At last Hallelujah lands on a tall shard of granite and holds a flight feather to his beak. "Make as little noise as possible," he says. "We don't want to wake up the river."

Steve and Sarah, nod, trying to pant quietly. When they can stand up straight again, Hallelujah points upward with one wing. Their eyes follow the wing up a large, old tree. There isn't much light, but they can just make out, as they squint and peer, the indistinct form of a naked woman crouched in a nest of twigs in the crotch of the tree. She appears to be sucking her thumb.

"Whoa," they say in unison, their mouths open and their arms at their sides.

"Maybe we should wake her up," says Sarah, not really sure she wants to.

"Two problems," says the owl. "One, the spell won't let her wake up, and two, there'd be no way for her to get down from the tree if she did."

"Oh," says Sarah, trying not to sound relieved.

Steve scratches his chin. "Hmm," he says. "Maybe—"

"I don't think so," says Hallelujah.

They walk back slowly, lost in their thoughts. Hallelujah sits on Sarah's shoulder.

"I don't want to sit on *your* shoulder," he says to Steve.

"Isn't there anything we can do?" asks Sarah.

"Certainly," says Hallelujah. "You could assemble a rescue party, if you think you can convince anyone the story is true. Or you could wrestle the river for three nights and days. Or—"

"Maybe she likes being an osprey," offers Steve.

Sarah and Hallelujah glower at him.

"Just a thought," he says.

"I'm sure you'll do the sensible thing," says the owl, once they're back at the campfire. "You'll sleep on it, worry about it for awhile, and then you'll come to the conclusion, without really talking about it, that she was never actually real. Or me either, for that matter. Not many people think I'm real, even those whose minds are open enough to hear more than garbled hootings coming from my beak."

Sarah thinks for a moment, then smiles. "You came to us because you knew we'd understand."

"Well," said the owl, "that, and I wanted a marshmallow." He lifts up his brow hopefully. Steve tosses over the bag.

"Oh, thank you!" says Hallelujah. He jumps on the bag and flies away with it, frighteningly, over their heads.

Sarah's breath hitches. "Good-bye!" she says.

The night is silent.

Steve and Sarah sit for awhile, staring at the flames

"Did you know about . . . things like that?" asks Sarah.

Steve shakes his head.

"Me neither."

"We're awake, right? I mean, we didn't . . ."

"I feel pretty awake. Our marshmallows are gone. And my legs hurt, like I've been running."

"True. True."

"How is it possible we didn't know about . . . "

Steve ponders. "It's like fairy tales, I guess. I mean, everyone's heard them, but we all assume they're just, you know, parables, or morality plays. Not, you know, actually true."

"Huh." Sarah ponders. "What do you suppose . . . ?"

"Is the moral of the osprey story?"

"Yeah."

"Good question."

"I feel like we should help her. Like . . . like the story isn't finished until we do."

"Yeah. I know what you mean."

"Should we talk to the river?"

Steve laughs, then stops laughing.

They stare into the flames for awhile.

An hour passes.

Then two.

Finally, Steve stands up and yawns, stretching his arms above his head. "Well—long day tomorrow. . . ."

"Yeah," says Sarah. "I bet they all are."

Some time later, the sun rises, as it has every morning, so far. The osprey opens one eye and shivers. The sunrise reminds her of something unpleasant, like dishes that should have been washed the night before. Not that she remembers what dishes are. She stretches her head down to preen some belly feathers, and her gaze sweeps over the strange familiarity of her nest. Hesitating briefly, she runs her beak through warm, soft underdown, then looks up, sharply, at the sun. Her eyes narrow, but she can't quite bring her suspicions into focus. Nearby, an owl repeats its single question.

She wishes she could answer.

Steve Holt stands on the bank of the river and judges the distance to the first wet rock. "You're a mean son of a bitch," he mutters, under his breath.

"What?" asks Sarah, from behind him.

"Nothing. Just . . ."

He hops to the first rock, and loses his balance, but manages to angle his fall so that his other foot lands on another rock. Straddling a cubit and a half of water, he mutters, "May the filth of a thousand . . ."

"What, honey? I can't hear you."

Steve shakes his head, unwilling to raise his voice above the tumbling mumblings of the river.

He navigates the next three rocks, then clambers safely up the far bank. He turns, and waits for Sarah to do the same, a strange fear gripping him as he watches.

Sarah duplicates his first maneuver and stands, waving her arms for balance, for three precarious seconds, then helplessly steps into the water.

Steve screams.

Slowly, inevitably, Sarah falls to her hands and knees.

The adrenaline in Steve's bloodstream shouts at him to run away, while his loyalty suggests he leap to his wife's defense. Trembling, he stands stock still.

The river flows on.

Slowly, awkwardly, Sarah stands up. She looks at her husband, sees his terror, and rolls her eyes. Then, to Steve's further horror, she lowers herself into a crouch.

His eyes wide, his mouth an "O," Steve raises his hands as if to cast a spell of stopping on her.

She jumps straight up and lands straight down, like a little girl stomping in a puddle.

Unsurprisingly, nothing happens, except that Steve gets splashed. While he sputters, Sarah wades over to him and climbs out of the water, smiling mischievously.

Feeling slightly sick, Steve manages nonetheless to laugh. Wagging his finger at the river, he says, "And there's more where that came from if you don't turn Emma back!"

Still laughing, they hook each other's arms and swagger off.

Surprisingly, the river is impressed. True, it's not the epic wrestling match that a hero of old might have managed, but at least they acknowledged his existence. With the swirl of an eddy he motions to the sun, who dapples through the leaves to show he's listening.

"I was going to anyway, eventually," says the river. "I mean, it's not like any toilets backed into me. Downstream may be another matter, but up here, well, I'm never the same river twice, you know."

"So you keep saying," says the sun.

"Anyway, you might want to make sure our feathered friend is near the ground before I break the curse. In five, four, three . . ."

Emma was never sure, afterwards, whether she truly regained her mind, but aside from an aversion to freshwater fish and an alarming fondness for spending the occasional night in a tree, she managed to live a reasonably normal life. Her husband, it turns out, had never entirely given her up for lost, and had taken a job as a forest ranger in the mad hope of someday hearing rumors of her whereabouts. When hikers began telling stories of a wild woman dancing naked through the forest, singing off key and off color, he was overjoyed, and derelict in his duties for days until his beloved and disheveled wife was once more in his arms, squawking and fretting, just like old times.

Steve and Sarah are still married, last I heard, and mostly happy, but they don't go hiking much anymore. They heard the story of Emma's return on the news, same as anybody, but they never tried to contact her. Occasionally, they build a bonfire in their back yard and invite some friends over to drink beer and smoke marijuana, and, late in the night, if they're drunk enough and the mood is mellow, they'll pop in a CD of Handel's *Messiah* and act out the story of an owl named Hallelujah, a woman-turned-osprey named Emma, and the three, harrowing, glorious days they spent tag-team wrestling a god.

www.ingramcontent.com/pod-product-compliance
Lightning Source LLC
Chambersburg PA
CBHW022023170626
46808CB00003B/1042